The
MYSTERY
of the
SINISTER
SCARECROW

It was almost dark. Suddenly The Three Investigators heard a scream.

"It's Letitia Radford!" cried Pete. He started sprinting up the hill to the big house.

Jupiter and Bob were right on his heels. The screaming went on.

"No!" the woman shrieked. "No. Don't! Please don't!"

The screaming stopped abruptly, and the boys heard violent weeping. And then, swooping down on them like a living nightmare, came a hideous scarecrow wielding a scythe!

Alfred Hitchcock
and The Three Investigators in

The
MYSTERY
of the
SINISTER
SCARECROW

Text by M. V. Carey

Based on characters created by Robert Arthur

Random House  New York

Library of Congress Cataloging in Publication Data
Carey, M V
   Alfred Hitchcock and the three investigators in
The mystery of the sinister scarecrow.

   (Alfred Hitchcock mystery series; no. 29)
   SUMMARY: The theft of some mutant army ants by a
scarecrow leads the Three Investigators to the
solution of two daring crimes in the art world.
   [1. Mystery and detective stories]   I. Arthur,
Robert. II. Title. III. Series.
PZ7.C213Ali [Fic]   79–10034
ISBN 0–394–84182–4 pbk.
ISBN 0–394–94182–9 lib. bdg.

Manufactured in the United States of America
  2 3 4 5 6 7 8 9 0

Contents

A Word from Alfred Hitchcock

Greetings, mystery lovers!

Once more I have the pleasure of introducing an adventure of The Three Investigators, those daring young sleuths who are always intrigued by the uncanny and the bizarre. In this case, the boys attempt to help a lady in distress. A worthy endeavor, you will say. Quite so. But it is a dangerous one, too! As the young detectives go about their task, they must match wits with a sinister scarecrow who haunts the twilight, and evade the killer ants that march in the night.

If you already know The Three Investigators, you may turn immediately to Chapter One, where the story begins. If you have not yet met this remarkable trio, be informed that Jupiter Jones, the leader of the group, is a stout lad with an encyclopedic memory and a marvelous talent for deduction. Pete Crenshaw, the second investigator, is quick and athletic—if occasionally alarmed at Jupiter's ability to stir up trouble. Bob Andrews is a studious boy whose skill as a researcher helps solve the puzzles that confront the boys. All three lads reside in Rocky Beach, California, a small town on the Pacific Coast not far from Hollywood.

So much for the introductions. Now on with the adventure!

ALFRED HITCHCOCK

The
MYSTERY
of the
SINISTER
SCARECROW

1

Attacked!

"Watch out!" yelled Pete Crenshaw. "We'll crash!"

The pickup truck from The Jones Salvage Yard skidded on the dirt road. Brakes screeched, let go, then screeched again. Then the truck jolted into the ditch and came to a bone-rattling halt with one fender crumpled against a live oak tree.

"By golly!" said Hans, the driver. He was one of two Bavarian brothers who worked in the salvage yard. He sat for a moment and drew a deep breath. Then again he said, "By golly!"

Hans took a careful look at the three boys in the truck. Jupiter Jones, sitting next to him in the cab, appeared shaken but unharmed. In the open back of the truck, Pete Crenshaw and Bob Andrews were still hanging on to the side for dear life. Their feet were braced to keep them from being thrown out.

"You okay?" called Hans.

Bob and Pete nodded and let go of the side of

the truck. Their muscles were cramped from holding on so tight.

Slowly everyone climbed out of the truck to inspect the damage. Hans stared with dismay at the front tire that had blown out, sending them careening off the winding mountain road.

"By golly!" said Hans for the third time. "I did not think I had been going so fast."

"Can you get her out of the ditch?" asked Jupiter.

Hans looked doubtful. He climbed back behind the wheel. The ignition ground and the engine roared. Gears shifted and Hans looked back over his shoulder. But the rear wheels of the truck spun uselessly in the dirt.

Hans killed the engine and climbed down again. "We are stuck," he said. "Jupe, I think we call your uncle Titus. He will come with the other truck and haul us out. Then I can change the tire."

"Oh, great!" said Pete. "Call him from where?"

Hans and the three boys looked around at the deserted landscape. They had left Rocky Beach twenty minutes earlier, bound for a cabin in the Santa Monica Mountains. The owner wanted to sell his belongings before he headed back to his hometown in Indiana.

"Some of the people who live in those hills have interesting things," Uncle Titus had said after he received the telephone call from the man. "Jupiter, why don't you and Hans or Konrad take the truck and go see what the man is selling? If his bed's really brass, as he says, buy it. And buy anything else you think we can resell."

"Nothing weird, please, Jupiter," said Aunt Mathilda Jones. She was always irritated when Uncle Titus came home from a buying trip with an item that would be difficult to dispose of. But her fears were groundless. The Jones Salvage Yard in Rocky Beach was known up and down the Pacific Coast. Buyers came there looking for items that could not be found anywhere else, so even the most unusual things were eventually sold.

Jupiter had been excited at the thought of doing some buying on his own. Until now Uncle Titus had done all the buying. Jupe had hurried to call his friends Bob and Pete. Then he had gone to look for Uncle Titus's helpers, Hans and his brother, Konrad. In less than half an hour Hans had the smaller of the two trucks ready to go.

Hans had driven north from Rocky Beach along the Coast Highway, and then had turned onto Chaparral Canyon Road, a broad, well-paved highway that led up over the mountains and then down the other side into the San Fernando Valley. Almost four miles into Chaparral Canyon, Hans had guided the truck to the right onto an unpaved, one-lane track called Rock Rim Drive. He had been only a few hundred yards down Rock Rim when the tire blew.

"Looks as if I may not get to go on a buying spree after all," said Jupiter with a sigh. "Looks as if we may wind up hiking back to Rocky Beach."

He stared glumly at the scrub brush that covered the slopes around them. To their left a weather-worn old house perched on the hillside right above the road. It was obviously abandoned. The lower windows were boarded up and the glass was missing from many of the ones upstairs.

"No phone there, that's for sure," said Pete.

"Hey!" Bob pointed up the hill behind the old house. Near the top, and to the boys' right, was a stand of eucalyptus trees with a bit of red-tile roof showing above them. "There's a house up there," he said. "Looks like a big place. It must face Chaparral Canyon."

"Perhaps we don't need to go that far," said Jupe. "See the old barn halfway up the hill? There are telephone wires leading to it. Possibly someone lives there, and if we take a shortcut across the cornfield—"

He stopped, a wondering look on his face.

"What's the matter?" asked Bob.

"The cornfield," said Jupiter. He leaned on the fence that edged the road and stared. "Who ever heard of a cornfield in the middle of the Santa Monica Mountains?"

The corn in the small field beside the road was tall and green in the hot August sun. The ears were growing plump, and the earth around the plants was dark with moisture. Someone had gone to great trouble to irrigate it. The ground sloped up sharply

from the road, and on the uphill side of the field a
scarecrow perched on a fence. It stared at the boys
with eyes that were black triangles on a burlap-sack
face.

Jupe shook his head. "It's an odd place for a
farm."

"Just be glad it's here," said Bob, "and that it has
a telephone. C'mon, let's go!"

"Let's not all go," said Jupe. "If the farmer sees us
all trooping through his cornfield, he might not like
it."

Pete sat down and leaned against a fence post.
"Okay," he said. "I vote that Jupe goes, since it's
uphill all the way. He could use the exercise."

Jupe grimaced. He was overweight and didn't
like to be reminded of the fact.

"Just so somebody goes," said Hans. He sounded
anxious.

"All right, all right," said Jupiter. He heaved
himself over the fence and started up through the
corn, which was almost as high as his head. Aware
that a cornfield in these mountains was a rarity, he
stepped with care. His progress through the field
was not silent. The corn rustled as he passed, and
his breathing became loud. The slope grew steeper
and steeper, and he had to bend almost double as
he climbed.

He looked up through the cornstalks and saw the
scarecrow again. It was quite close now. He could
see the face clearly. The mouth seemed to grin at

him—a crooked grin.

"Another few yards," said Jupe to himself, "and I'll be in the clear."

He began to straighten up. Suddenly something large and dark hurtled at him from higher on the hill.

"You blasted *thing*!" shrieked a thin, furious voice. "I'll knock your head off!"

Jupe's breath went out in a gasp and his feet slid from under him. A raging, wild-eyed man collided with him, knocking him backward.

An instant later Jupe lay amid crushed cornstalks. He looked up at blue sky and green corn—and at a man like a black shadow kneeling on him, pressing a hand against his throat, threatening to crush the life out of him. The man's free hand was held high, and it clutched a nasty, jagged piece of rock!

2

The Bug Man

"Mister, please!" Jupe managed a husky croak.

The man let go of Jupe's throat. "Why . . . why, you're just a kid!" he exclaimed.

There was a sound of something crashing through the corn. Feet pounded on the soft earth, and then Jupe saw, against the sky, the huge, comforting bulk of Hans.

"You do not do that to Jupiter!" declared Hans. He lifted the man bodily off Jupiter and threw him aside, sending him rolling a short way down the hill. "I will break you into pieces!" he threatened.

Jupe got slowly to his feet. He saw the man who had attacked him blinking up at Hans. He had the squinting, searching look of an extremely nearsighted person, and he was feeling around in the dirt.

"My glasses!" he said. There was a note of annoyance in his voice. "I dropped my glasses!"

Bob and Pete had hurried up the hill with Hans.

9

Now Bob stooped and picked a pair of aviator-style thick-lensed glasses from among the crushed cornstalks. He handed the glasses to the man, who wiped them on the front of his denim shirt and put them on. Then the man stood up and dusted off his blue jeans.

"What is the matter with you?" demanded Hans. "Are you a crazy man that you want to hit Jupiter?"

"I'm very sorry," said the man stiffly, as if he were unused to acknowledging his mistakes. "I'm sorry, but I thought you were the scarecrow and—"

The man stopped. He looked over at the scarecrow perched on the fence, grinning its lopsided grin.

"I mean . . . uh . . . we've had some trouble here with trespassers. They trample the corn and . . . and make trouble generally and . . . and I'm afraid I overreacted when I s_ _hat someone was coming up the hill."

The man paused. His bald head gleamed in the sunlight. His eyes were pale behind his thick lenses. Jupe saw that the man was not large. He was scarcely taller than Jupe himself, and quite thin. But he was muscular and suntanned, like someone who spent long hours out of doors and got plenty of exercise. Jupe guessed that he was in his late thirties.

"I wouldn't really have hit you with that rock," the bald man said to Jupe. "I just wanted to see who you were."

"You thought I was a scarecrow," said Jupe.

"Oh, no! No, of course not! Ridiculous! You must have misunderstood me. Now, would you kindly tell me what you are all doing in my cornfield?"

Jupe blinked at how quickly the man had seized the offensive again. Then he nodded and began to explain. "Our truck blew a tire and ran into the ditch down on Rock Rim Drive. I saw the telephone wires leading to the barn up there, and I wanted to ask if I could call my uncle to come and pull us out of the ditch. I was just taking a shortcut through the cornfield."

"I see," said the man. "Well, I'm sorry I jumped on you, and yes, you can use the telephone."

He turned and started up the hill. The boys and Hans followed him through a gate in the fence and across a stretch of grass to the old red barn. The bald man opened the big center door, switched on overhead fluorescent lights, and waved his visitors inside.

There was no sign of any animals or farming machines in the big building. Instead, there were long tables on which strange equipment stood in a sort of orderly clutter. Before Jupe could take a closer look, he was led to a desk on one side of the barn.

"Go ahead and make your call," said the man. He pointed to a telephone half buried by piles of books and notebooks on the desk.

While Jupe called home, Bob, Pete, and Hans

looked around curiously. On the long table nearest the entrance they saw several wooden frames about a foot square. The frames had cheesecloth tacked to one side and panes of glass covering the other side. They looked like shadowbox picture frames, but they were empty. A camera mounted on a floor dolly was focused downward on one of the frames.

Several large glass jars stood on another table. Bob peered into one jar and saw what looked like shreds of moss inside. Then, with a shock, he realized that they were not shreds of moss. They were living chains of ants—brown, long-legged ants that clung to one another with their legs and jaws. Bob stared hard at the insects, fascinated and a little repulsed.

Jupiter hung up the telephone. "Everything's arranged," he announced. "Uncle Titus will meet us down on Rock Rim Drive within half an hour."

"Very good," said the bald man. He moved as if to usher his visitors outside, but was stopped by Bob's wondering voice.

"Do you collect *ants*?"

"Yes. Yes, I do," said the man. Some warmth crept into his voice for the first time. "But I don't just collect them. I observe them and note what they do. Then I try to decide what they'll do next. I keep watching them, and eventually I find out if I'm right."

"You're an entomologist," said Jupiter.

The man smiled. "Not many people your age know that word."

"Jupe reads a lot," Pete explained. "We don't know what he's talking about half the time. What did he call you, an ento . . . etom—?"

"An entomologist," said the man. "That's a scientist who studies insects, and yes, I am one. My name is Woolley, Dr. Charles Woolley. I've written several books about army ants. I'm working on a book now, but I don't know the ending."

Woolley grinned, and it occurred to Jupe that he might be a pleasant person when he wanted to be. The thought also came to Jupe that Woolley's head was really too large for his thin body, and that the eyes behind the thick lenses protruded slightly. With a bald dome and a face that tapered to a pointed chin, Woolley actually resembled an ant. Jupe stared at the man's forehead, almost expecting antennae to appear there.

Woolley put his hand to his head. "What's the matter?" he asked. "Is there something on me?"

Jupe started. "Oh, no. No, I was just thinking about your book. If you don't know the ending, I deduce that you haven't finished your studies of the insects here. This is your laboratory, isn't it?"

"The entire hillside is my laboratory," said Woolley. "This barn is where I do special studies. Those frames you see keep ants confined while I photograph them. The camera above the table has a magnifying lens. I have a darkroom over in the corner. The ants you see in the jars were taken from a colony that lives in the little greenhouse behind this barn. At least that's where the colony lives right now. They may soon decide to move somewhere else. They're about due to migrate."

"When they migrate, will you know the ending of the book?" Bob asked. "Where will they migrate to?"

"Probably they won't go far," said Woolley. "They may go up the hill nearer the big house. Since they're army ants, we call the place where they nest a bivouac—a camp. Ants are much like bees. The entire colony depends on the queen. When she's about to lay eggs, she's huge, so the colony stays in one place and the worker ants go out every day to find food. After the queen lays her eggs she's slim again and able to move, and the colony can migrate. The colony that's in the greenhouse has migrated several times since I came here. A great stream of army ants marching along is an impressive sight, let me tell you!"

Jupiter frowned. "I didn't know we had army ants in this country," he said. "I've read horror stories about the army ants in Africa. Aren't they the ones that march into native villages and eat everything in sight, including large animals?"

Woolley nodded cheerfully. "Absolutely everything," he said. "Most ants are vegetarians, but army ants are carnivorous—they're predatory nomads. The Africans call their army ants 'the visitors,' and they run when a colony heads their way. The ants could easily eat a human—and have!"

Pete shuddered, but Woolley continued talking

enthusiastically, unaffected by the horrible picture he'd painted.

"The ants have their uses, though. They eat rats and centipedes and anything else they find. When the Africans return to their villages after a raid by army ants, they find nice clean houses that have no vermin in them.

"The army ants we have on this continent aren't as ferocious as the African ants. They will eat small animals if they can, but for the most part they live on other insects. They're more widespread than you'd suppose. One species is found all through Panama and Mexico. There's another type in the United States. It might be found anywhere south of forty-five degrees latitude. That's as far north as Oregon and Maine.

"And then there are the ants here on this hillside. They aren't exactly the sort of army ants you'd expect to find here. Their legs are longer than the ones that have previously been seen in this area, and their body armor is thicker."

Woolley paused for a moment, and his face lit up with excitement. "Want to see something amazing?" he asked.

He didn't wait for an answer, but opened the door and went out. Hans and the boys followed him up the hill.

"This land belongs to Chester Radford," said Woolley. "You may know of him. He's very wealthy, and he's generous. He supports a lot of scientific work. I was hiking near here last spring when I spotted some strange army ants. I confirmed that they were unusual, and also that they were on the Radford estate. Mr. Radford lives abroad, but I was able to contact him. He gave me permission to live here and use the barn for a workshop. He also authorized a grant from the Radford Fund for Further Education in the Sciences, so I can carry on my work."

Woolley stopped in front of a small greenhouse, which had about it a neglected and abandoned air. The door to the little building creaked when the scientist opened it.

"Now, here is a colony of army ants!"

Charles Woolley knelt and pointed to a dark, bulging mass of material that hung from the underside of a table. It moved slightly in the draft from the open door. The motion reminded Jupiter of the way fur moves when someone blows on it. The mass was a huge, seething bundle of ants, all clinging to one another.

"Yuck!" said Pete.

"Fascinating, aren't they?" said Woolley. "And not quite like any other army ants I've seen. Perhaps a new subspecies. Perhaps mutants. How long have they been here? Where did they come from? Where are they going? These are the questions I'm trying to answer."

Hans looked worriedly at the mass of tiny creatures. "I think we better go," he said. "Mr. Jones will be here any minute."

He went out, and after a minute the boys followed him. Skirting the cornfield, they picked their way down through the scrub brush on the hill toward Rock Rim Drive. Once Jupe looked back. Woolley was standing near the cornfield fence watching them. The scarecrow on the fence seemed to watch, too, with its blank triangle eyes and a grin that was a bit menacing.

"Strange guy," said Pete. "He's really nuts about ants!"

"That's not what's strange," said Jupe. "What's strange is that a serious scientist mistook me for a living scarecrow!"

3

Strangers Step In

"Well, all I know is that it's more than five miles from here to the turnoff at Rock Rim Drive," said Pete, "and most of it is uphill. Now, why should I pump a bike for five miles in the hottest part of the day just to take another look at that scarecrow?"

It was several hours after the boys' adventure on the hillside of the Radford estate. Jupiter, Pete, and Bob were sitting in a booth at the Seaview Cafe in Rocky Beach, eating ice cream and talking over the events of the morning. Jupe had just explained that he'd excused himself from the second attempt at a buying trip in the mountains. Uncle Titus was going to the cabin himself, because Jupe wanted to return to the strange cornfield instead. Pete and Bob weren't enthusiastic about the change in plans.

"Have you no curiosity?" said Jupiter. His tone was reproachful. "Don't you want to investigate that sinister scarecrow?"

"It isn't sinister," Pete declared. "It's just a bunch of old clothes."

"All right, but why did Charles Woolley think he saw a live scarecrow on the hill?" Jupe demanded. "Why did he attack me?"

"I think you're making a big mystery out of nothing," said Bob. "Woolley just got excited, that's all."

Jupe shook his head. "No, that isn't all. Because he got too excited. How many people get really violent with a trespasser? Woolley had a rock in his hand. If he'd hit me with that, he could have fractured my skull.

"And yet I don't think he's really a violent person. Once he saw who I was, he calmed down. It was only when he thought I was a thing that he was so furious. Remember, he called me a blasted thing! As if I weren't a human being! That isn't natural. If he'd called me a sneak or a crook, I wouldn't have paid attention. But he called me a thing! Then, when he apologized, he said he'd mistaken me for the scarecrow."

Pete chuckled. "You're too fat to be a scarecrow," he said.

A young man in a short-sleeved shirt and dark trousers had been sipping a cup of coffee at the counter that ran along one side of the cafe. He turned now and looked at Jupe. "You *are* too hefty to be the scarecrow," he said. "Too short, too."

The three boys gaped at the man. He picked up

his coffee cup and came to their table. Pete moved over to make room for him in the booth.

"I hope you're talking about the scarecrow up on Chaparral Canyon Road," said the man. "The one who wanders around the Radford place. I couldn't stand it if there were more than one walking scarecrow in the world!"

"You mean the scarecrow does walk?" said Jupe.

The man nodded. He was enjoying the sensation he had created. "I saw him," he told the boys. "My name's Conklin. Larry Conklin. I work for the Safe-T-System Company. My firm makes burglar alarm systems, and we install and service them. We did the system at the Mosby Museum up on Chaparral Canyon."

Jupiter nodded. "I know the place."

"Fabulous, isn't it?" said Larry Conklin. "I hear old Millionaire Mosby, who built it, wanted his house to be stronger than any fortress. It needs to be, too. It's filled with fine paintings from all over the world. We've got the place wired with a super alarm system. And we check it at least once a week to make sure it's operating right."

"But what about the scarecrow?" said Jupiter.

"Oh, yes. Well, I was at the Mosby place one evening a week or so ago, and just as I was getting into my car to leave, I saw a scarecrow go scooting around the side of the Radford house. That's right across the road. I only saw the scarecrow for a second. Then it ran down the hill and disappeared."

Larry Conklin paused and sipped his coffee.

"And then?" prompted Jupiter.

"Then nothing," said Conklin. "I thought I was seeing things. It was dusk and the light was tricky. I stood still and sort of replayed the scene in my mind like an instant replay on television. And I could see it just as clear. It was a scarecrow, all right. But I sure wasn't about to ring the doorbell at the Mosby house and report a scarecrow loose in the neighborhood. They'd have thought I was batty!"

"They sure would!" said Pete.

"So I was glad to hear you boys talking just now," said Conklin. He stared at Jupe. "Somebody mistook you for the scarecrow, huh? You don't look at all like him."

"I was coming through a cornfield," said Jupe. "The person who made the mistake couldn't see me clearly."

"That figures," said Conklin.

"What did your scarecrow look like?" Bob asked.

Conklin frowned. "Oh, medium height. Maybe five foot seven or eight. Thin. He had a black hat and a light-colored jacket. I couldn't make out his features; the face was just a blob. He had straw sticking out of his sleeves. That's how I knew he was a scarecrow."

Conklin finished his coffee and stood up. "I don't go poking into things that aren't my business," he said, "and maybe you boys shouldn't, either. There was something kind of nasty about that scarecrow.

Why don't you just forget the whole thing?"

The boys didn't answer, and Conklin went out of the cafe.

Jupiter looked slyly at Pete and Bob. "Do you want to forget the whole thing?"

"Yeah! But you won't let us," said Pete. "So let's go. It's a long ride up to that cornfield."

The three boys got their bikes from the rack outside the cafe, and soon were pedaling north on the Coast Highway. They turned onto Chaparral Canyon and labored up the grade into the mountains.

When they came to the place where Rock Rim Drive forked off to the right, Pete stopped and waited for Bob and Jupe to catch up with him.

"Do we go in through the cornfield, the way we did this morning?" he said.

"I'm not anxious to irritate Dr. Woolley any more today," said Jupiter. "Look ahead. Isn't that a dirt road that cuts across the Radford property and runs down the hill to the cornfield?"

"We might irritate Dr. Woolley almost as much on a dirt road," Bob pointed out.

"At least we wouldn't seem to be furtive," said Jupiter. He led the way up Chaparral Canyon to the point where an unpaved track crossed the Radford land. From there the boys could see the barn halfway down the hill where Woolley conducted his studies. To the left of the barn, and a little uphill, stood the greenhouse that sheltered the seething, pulsating colony of ants. Beyond the greenhouse was a row of eucalyptus trees running straight across the slope. The dirt road ended at the trees.

Jupe looked ahead along Chaparral Canyon. He saw a stately, L-shaped white house with a red tile roof. In the angle formed by the two wings of the house, a swimming pool was set into a terrace. All around the house were velvety lawns.

Across the road from this elegant residence there was an oddly fashioned, windowless building. It was made entirely of concrete.

"The Mosby place," said Pete. "That's a nutty building. And this is a nutty place for a museum, up in these hills."

"It was Mosby's home when Mosby was alive," said Jupiter. "A lot of wealthy people live up here. At least the building is functional. Since it houses a great art collection, the fact that it has no windows is a real advantage. It is absolutely secure."

"It's also ugly," said Bob. "I'll bet the Radfords had a fit when it was built!"

The boys began to wheel their bikes down the dusty road toward the eucalyptus trees. They were quiet now. Into the mind of each came the picture of Charles Woolley as they had first seen him that morning, raging and threatening.

When they reached the trees the boys could see the scarecrow and the cornfield. Leaving their bikes, they walked down to the rail fence along the field and looked closely at the scarecrow.

The thing had no legs. It was supported by a stick nailed to the fence. A second stick fastened at right angles to the first one made the arms. The scarecrow wore a black hat, a faded corduroy jacket with straw stuffed in the arms, and old gray work gloves. Its head was a straw-filled burlap sack tied at the neck with string. Black triangles had been painted on for eyes, and a black slash for a grinning mouth.

"It couldn't walk," said Jupe. "Not possibly."

There was a gasp. The boys looked around. A woman stood on a path that led away through the eucalyptus trees. At first glance she looked as if she'd just stepped out of an ad for some expensive product. She had a thin, aristocratic face and wore a casually elegant costume of blue silk slacks and a printed silk overblouse. But a closer look showed faded blond hair, drawn features, and haunted eyes.

The woman stared at the boys. "What did you say?" she demanded of Jupe.

"I said—" Jupe began boldly enough, but then stopped. It would sound ridiculous to repeat his statement that the scarecrow couldn't walk, and Jupiter hated to sound ridiculous.

"You said it couldn't walk," said the woman. Her voice was raised now, and there was an edge to it, as if she could barely control herself. "What do you know about this scarecrow?"

"Nothing, really," said Jupiter. "We met a man in town who said he saw a scarecrow walking around up here. That sounded strange, so we came to have a look for ourselves."

"A man saw the scarecrow?" The woman's face was eager. "What man? Where is he?"

Jupiter hesitated. Larry Conklin worked for the firm responsible for the safety of the Mosby Museum. What would his superiors think if they learned that Conklin was telling a strange tale of a scarecrow seen running through the dusk?

"Well?" the woman demanded.

"The man was just a passerby," said Jupe. "We don't really know him. He said he saw the scarecrow up near the Radford house."

"I knew it!" cried the woman. She laughed hysterically. "There really is a scarecrow who walks! He's real! I have a witness!"

And she put her hands to her face and burst into tears.

4

The Crazy Woman

The boys stared aghast at the sobbing woman. They didn't know what to do. Fortunately she calmed down quickly, and looked at the boys with some embarrassment.

"I'm sorry," she said. "You must think I'm crazy. But then everybody thinks I'm crazy. But I'm not, am I? The scarecrow *does* wander around!"

Jupe looked skeptically at the legless scarecrow.

"Well, of course, it mightn't have been *that* scarecrow," said the woman. "Maybe it's another one that just looks like that scarecrow."

Jupiter grinned cautiously. "You mean that perhaps this scarecrow has a twin?"

"Who cares?" said the woman. "Just so that someone's seen one walk! Would you mind coming up to the house with me? I'd like you to tell Mrs. Chumley that I wasn't imagining it all."

"There isn't much we can tell anyone," said Jupiter.

"Then you can just get off this property!" said the
woman sharply. "What are you doing here anyway?
It isn't your business!"

"That's true," said Jupe, unperturbed. "But a
scarecrow who walks is an interesting puzzle. We
like puzzles."

Jupe opened his wallet, took out a card, and
handed it to her. It read:

THE THREE INVESTIGATORS
"We Investigate Anything"
? ? ?

First Investigator . . . . Jupiter Jones
Second Investigator . . . . Peter Crenshaw
Records and Research . . . . Bob Andrews

"I don't understand," said the woman.

"We are private investigators," said Jupiter.

"You can't be!" said the woman.

"But we are," Jupe declared. He spoke in his
most serious, grown-up way. "As the question
marks on our card indicate, we find the unknown
intriguing. And we do not regard anyone's ideas as
completely outrageous. Not before we investigate
them. That's why we've been quite successful with
cases that have baffled more conventional agencies."

"I believe you mean it," said the woman. "All
right, I'll pay you. Come up to the house and tell
Mrs. Chumley that the scarecrow walks and I'll
make it worth your while."

Jupiter looked at his friends. "We don't want

money just for repeating a man's story, do we?"

"Nope," said Bob.

"Well, come on, then," said the woman.

She started up the path toward the house, and The Three Investigators fell into step beside her.

"Who is Mrs. Chumley?" asked Pete.

"She was my mother's social secretary, and now she looks after the house for us," said the woman. "I'm Letitia Radford, by the way. I live here. Sometimes. When I'm not someplace else."

"And you saw the scarecrow walk?" prompted Jupe.

"Several times," said the woman. "I think he . . . he comes looking for me. At dusk. Always at dusk."

They were clear of the trees now, and crossing the lawn. "No one else ever sees him," she went on. "They think I'm mad! They think I imagine it."

She stopped. There was a look of fear and disgust on her face. "I hate scarecrows. And bugs. I detest bugs!"

She shuddered. "Never mind. Just come and tell Mrs. Chumley what you told me. She's got me seeing a psychiatrist in Beverly Hills. Sure that I've gone round the bend."

Miss Radford walked on across the lawn and went up several brick steps to the terrace at the side of the Radford mansion. The boys followed, and looked with admiration at the huge swimming pool that they had first noticed from the road. A table had been set for two near the pool. A slender, sandy-haired man in a white jacket hovered by it, as if checking to see that everything was in order.

"Burroughs, where is Mrs. Chumley?" demanded Letitia Radford.

"She's in her room, miss," said the man. He had a British accent. "Mrs. Burroughs has gone to help her. She said—"

"Never mind. Here she is."

A woman in a black uniform and a white apron pushed a wheelchair through a door onto the terrace. In the chair sat a woman who appeared to be in her sixties. Her white hair was crimped into curls and her faded cheeks were rouged. Her legs were covered with a crocheted afghan.

"Ah, Letitia! There you are, dear," she said. Her dark, sparkling eyes rested on the boys. "And who are these young men?" she inquired.

"These boys are called The Three Investigators, Mrs. Chumley," said Letitia Radford. She looked at the card Jupe had given her. Then she glanced at Jupe. "I assume that you're Jupiter Jones, First Investigator," she said.

"That's right," said Jupe.

"And I suppose the boy with the muscles is Pete Crenshaw," she went on, "because I think the boy with the glasses must be Bob Andrews, who does all the research."

Bob grinned. "You have it right."

"I found these boys investigating the scarecrow

that that nut Woolley put up by his cornfield," said Letitia Radford, "and guess what!"

"What, dear?" said the woman in the wheelchair.

"The boys were curious because a man they met in town saw the scarecrow running around here!"

Letitia's tone was triumphant, but Mrs. Chumley seemed only politely interested. "Perhaps the boys will stay to tea and tell us about it," she said. "Burroughs, will you set three more places?"

"Certainly," said the man in the white jacket.

He and Mrs. Burroughs went into the house, and Mrs. Chumley wheeled herself to the tea table.

"So you met a man who saw a scarecrow running about," she said to the boys. "How very remarkable. Do sit down and tell us everything."

Jupiter took a seat next to Mrs. Chumley. "It is remarkable," he agreed. He had no time to say more, for Charles Woolley was coming up the steps from the lawn. His eyes, behind his thick glasses, were fixed on the boys in an accusing way.

"What is going on here?" demanded the bald scientist.

"We are about to have tea, Dr. Woolley," said Letitia Radford coldly. "Did you want something?"

Woolley stamped forward. "You and your broken-down truck!" he said to the boys. "You were lying! You just wanted an excuse to get into my laboratory and . . . and . . ."

The scientist stopped, unsure what to say next.

"To get into your laboratory and do what?" asked

Jupe. "We made a telephone call and that's all. Then, oddly enough, we met a man who saw a scarecrow walking around up here. We understand that Miss Radford sees it, too. She says she's the only one here who does see it. Is that true, Dr. Woolley?"

Charles Woolley didn't answer, but his face flushed.

"*You've* seen it!" cried Letitia Radford. She jumped up. "You've seen it, haven't you!"

"Well, actually, I did see something," admitted Charles Woolley, uncomfortably. "The night that I called the police—the night someone broke into my lab. I caught a glimpse of something that looked like a scarecrow."

"But you said it was just a prowler!" said Letitia.

"I didn't want to upset you," said Woolley. "Besides, I'd had enough trouble with the police already. I mean, Chief Reynolds came from Rocky Beach with the officer who answered my call, and you should have seen his expression when I told him that a scarecrow had gotten into my lab, hit me on the head, and stolen a jar filled with ants."

Letitia Radford laughed. "How marvelous!" she cried. "He thought you were crazy! But why didn't you say anything to me? Everyone in this house has been thinking *I'm* crazy. Why didn't you tell me? How could you be so cruel?"

Woolley replied angrily, "I have my reputation as a scientist to consider, you know. I can't afford to be involved with freaky things. I'm engaged in important research!"

"O-ooh!" cried Letitia Radford. "You disgust me!" She turned and ran into the house. Mrs. Chumley looked after her with concern.

Woolley sighed. "Protect me from hysterical women!" he said. He turned to the boys. "You still haven't explained what you're doing here."

"We were examining the scarecrow," Jupe told him. "After you mistook me for a scarecrow this morning, we thought we'd better investigate."

"This morning you were trespassing," accused Woolley. "Now you're snooping."

"If you suspect us of something bad, why don't you call Chief Reynolds?" Bob suggested. "He knows us."

"I'll do that," said Woolley. He raised his voice. "Burroughs, kindly bring me a telephone!"

In a moment the houseman appeared with a telephone. He plugged it into a jack beside the door, handed the instrument to Woolley, and went away again. Woolley got Chief Reynolds of the Rocky Beach Police Department on the line.

"This is Dr. Charles Woolley calling from the Radford estate," he said crisply. "Three boys have been wandering in and out of here all day looking at our scarecrow and I wondered . . ."

He paused.

"Well, yes, one of them is rather chubby," he said.

After another pause he looked at Jupe. "You're Jupiter Jones?"

Jupe nodded.

Charles Woolley spoke into the telephone. "That's right. It's Jupiter Jones."

He listened again, then thanked the chief and hung up.

"Chief Reynolds asked me to tell you to stay out of trouble," he said. "He says there's no harm in you. In fact, he thinks you're all right. I'm the one he's not sure about."

At that instant a scream began inside the house. It was high and shrill and it went on and on.

"Good heavens!" cried Mrs. Chumley. "That's Letitia! *Now* what's happened?"

5

A Nasty Shock

Woolley and The Three Investigators found Letitia
Radford crouched back against a wall in the upstairs
hallway. "Ants!" she cried. She pointed to a door.
"In there! Millions of ants!"

"Good grief!" said Woolley. He opened the door,
and he and the boys darted through into a pretty
little sitting room. Beyond this was a big, square
bedroom with a huge fourposter bed. And on the
bed, scurrying busily to and fro, were hundreds of
ants!

Woolley stopped short and stared as if he couldn't
decide what to do next.

"Mrs. Burroughs!" screamed Letitia from the
landing outside. "Bug spray, Mrs. Burroughs!
Quick!"

"Could those be your missing ants?" said Jupe.

Woolley walked forward and peered at the ants
on the bed. "They certainly could be."

"Here now! What's all this?" said a hearty voice behind them.

The boys turned.

Mrs. Burroughs had appeared in the doorway. She had a can of insect spray in her hand. Letitia Radford hovered just behind her.

"Step aside, if you please," said Mrs. Burroughs. "I'll take care of those nasty things straightaway."

There was a cheerful, no-nonsense air about Mrs. Burroughs, and more than a hint of cockney accent in her speech. She bustled forward with great determination and began to spray the ants.

"Now don't you worry, miss," she advised Letitia Radford. "We'll get these horrid little fellows out of the way and then I'll change the linens and you'll be all clean and comfy, just as if nothing had ever happened."

Letitia glared at Woolley. "It's your fault!" she accused. "We never had bugs in the house before you came with your cameras and jars and plastic tubes and . . ."

"My dear Letitia," said Woolley, "the ants were out on the hillside before I ever came. As to their coming into the house—"

"They didn't come in," said Jupe. "They were carried in."

He stooped and picked up a jar which had fallen partly under the bed. There were a few ants inside it. "Is this yours?" he asked Woolley.

The scientist nodded. "It looks like the one that

was taken by the scarecrow the other night."

Jupiter grinned happily. "A thieving scarecrow! Better and better. This case is getting really interesting!"

"You needn't sound so happy about it!" cried Letitia Radford. Now there were angry red spots in her pale cheeks. "You can just get out!" She turned on Woolley. "You, too! Take your horrible ants and go! I'm calling my brother tonight. You'll be off this place by tomorrow!"

"There now!" Mrs. Burroughs used the tone one might use to soothe a temperamental child. She put the insect spray down, then pulled the bedspread up and folded it over the dead ants. She handed the ant-filled spread to Woolley.

"Off with you now," she said. "Take 'em out of here. We can sort out who did it later on."

Woolley meekly took the spread and left. The Three Investigators followed him out and down the stairs.

The scientist paused in the lower hall and looked ruefully at the boys. "Looks like you're off the case," he said. "I just hope I'm not off my research project. Letitia is always ordering people out for one reason or another. Half the time she forgets about it as soon as her temper cools. We'll see if she really does call her brother tonight."

He shrugged and went out the front door, carrying the bedspread full of ants. The boys walked through the living room of the big house and out onto the terrace. Mrs. Chumley was still there, drinking her tea, as unruffled as if an invasion of army ants were an everyday event. The Investigators told her they couldn't stay for tea after all. Mrs. Chumley looked politely regretful and said goodbye.

The boys returned to Rocky Beach just in time for supper. They had no chance to discuss the strange events of the day until they met the next morning in Jupe's workshop.

This was a corner of The Jones Salvage Yard that was partitioned off with carefully arranged heaps of junk. It was sheltered from the weather by an overhanging roof that ran around the perimeter of the yard and protected especially valuable items. The workshop contained the printing press that Jupe had fixed up with odd bits and pieces from the yard. Also in the workshop were a lathe, a band saw, and a drill press, as well as Jupe's swivel chair and workbench.

Jupe was sitting in the chair staring at nothing when Pete and Bob came into the workshop.

"Wondering about the scarecrow?" asked Bob.

"Aren't you?" answered Jupiter.

"Sure. And the ants. Who would steal a bunch of ants and put them in a lady's bed?"

"Someone who didn't like the lady," said Pete. "Maybe she's not easy to like. She has a nasty temper."

Pete stopped. A light over the printing press was

blinking on and off—a signal that the telephone was ringing in Headquarters.

Headquarters for the young detectives was an old mobile home trailer not far from Jupe's workshop. It was hidden from curious eyes by piles of odds and ends for which there was almost no demand. Uncle Titus had given the boys the trailer to use as a clubhouse, and then had forgotten about it. The Three Investigators were careful not to remind him.

"Aha!" said Jupiter when he saw the light. "I thought we might be getting a call this morning."

Pete stepped behind the printing press and tugged aside an iron grating that covered the opening of a section of corrugated pipe. Followed by the others, he crawled through the pipe, which was padded with odd pieces of carpeting. This was Tunnel Two, one of several secret passageways that led to the hidden trailer. The tunnel ran beneath some rusted iron beams to an opening directly under Headquarters. Pete pushed up a trap door in the trailer floor and scrambled into the office of The Three Investigators.

The telephone was still ringing. Pete answered it, listened for a moment, then grinned. "No, this is Pete," he said, "but Jupe's here and so is Bob."

He listened again. Then he said, "I'll see," and he covered the mouthpiece with his hand.

"Guess who this is!" he said.

"Letitia Radford," said Jupe. "She wants us to find out who is persecuting her in a scarecrow disguise and who put ants in her bed."

"Even a genius can be wrong," Pete declared happily. "It's Charles Woolley, and *he* wants us to find out who is persecuting Letitia and who put ants in her bed. He wants us to come and see him. He got our telephone number from Chief Reynolds."

"Well, well, well!" said Jupiter. "We have a case after all! I can go. Bob, how about you?"

Bob nodded.

"We're leaving right now!" said Pete into the telephone.

6

The Time Bomb

In less than an hour The Three Investigators were in the big red barn on the Radford estate.

"Letitia did not call her brother last night," announced Woolley with relief. He sat on a high stool and leaned his elbows on a table where trowels and tweezers and forceps were laid out neatly. "Not that Chester Radford would necessarily have listened to her. But I've been thinking. I can't ignore this scarecrow business any longer. It's not just Letitia's problem any more. It's mine, too. Someone is now using *my* ants to persecute her. I can't afford to have my research project jeopardized.

"I called Chief Reynolds this morning," the scientist went on, "and told him about yesterday's incident with the ants. I also told him that Letitia had seen the scarecrow several times. The chief didn't take any of it seriously. He thinks it amounts to nothing more than a neighborhood kid playing pranks on us. Said it was a perfect case for you boys to take on."

"And what do you think?" asked Jupiter. "Could some kid be playing a prank?"

"There are no kids in this neighborhood," said Woolley. "The Radford house and the Mosby Museum are the only homes within a couple of miles. You've met everyone who lives in the Radford house. Over at the Mosby place there's Gerhart Malz, who is the curator, and a couple of guards who double as maintenance men and who go home every night at five. Malz lives at the museum, but he's not a prankish type."

"I see," said Jupe. "Very well. If you wish to have The Three Investigators take you as a client, perhaps you had better begin at the beginning and tell us as much as you know about the case. The solution to the identity of the scarecrow may be simple. It may only take an outsider—one who isn't emotionally involved—to figure it out."

Bob took a notebook and a pen out of his pocket and prepared to take notes.

"Well, I'm the one responsible for the scarecrow," said Woolley. "I mean the one out there on the fence. I made him with old clothes that Mrs. Burroughs found in the Radford attic. I also planted the cornfield, just to make sure the ants wouldn't run out of food. You have no idea how many insects that cornfield attracts.

"The ants are what brought me here, as you

know. You could say they're my only interest. I don't spend much time at the big house, so I haven't become greatly involved with the lives of the people there. In addition to the grant that Chester Radford arranged, I have the use of this barn as a lab, and I am the nonpaying tenant in a guest house here on the grounds."

"Guest house?" said Jupe. "Where is that?"

"It's a small cottage some distance behind the big house," said Woolley. "Further over on the hill. You wouldn't have noticed it yesterday. There's a stand of oak trees between it and the Radford mansion."

"You have a nice arrangement," said Jupe. "I can understand why you wouldn't want to leave here."

"I certainly wouldn't," said Woolley. "I'm on a leave of absence from my faculty post at U.C.L.A., and it would be very awkward if I had to stop my work here. And I don't want to stop. Everything was going so well—until Letitia came home."

Bob looked up from his notes. "She was away when you first began your work here?" he asked.

"Yes, she was," said Woolley. "I came up in May and Letitia showed up in June. You probably don't know about Letitia, but she's a real jet-setter. She spends most of her time in Europe. But when she has man trouble, she runs home."

"When she has what?" said Pete.

Woolley smiled. "She's famous for her romances. She's been engaged many times, but she never gets

married. The engagement is always broken. Something always goes wrong. Then Letitia comes home
to the Santa Monica Mountains to rest and mend
her broken heart. Right now she's trying to forget
some Hungarian count.

"Letitia doesn't like insects, as I'm sure you've
noticed. So she wasn't happy when she found me on
the property studying ants. And when she began to
see the scarecrow, she connected it with me, no
doubt because I made the one on the fence."

"Has she seen it often?" asked Jupiter.

"Five times, I think. It drives her frantic. Once it
flung some insects at her, and Mrs. Chumley
thought she would lose her mind. Of course, no one
believed that she was really seeing a scarecrow.
Mrs. Chumley insisted that she start seeing a
psychiatrist in Beverly Hills. But since the scarecrow *is* real, the doctor isn't much help."

"Tell me about Mrs. Chumley," said Jupe. "She
acts like—"

"Like the real lady of the house," said Woolley.
"She sure does. She was the social secretary to Mrs.
Harrison Radford, Letitia's mother. Mrs. Radford
died several years ago—long after her husband
died—and Mrs. Chumley had her accident at about
that time. She fell into the swimming pool, which
was empty because it was being repaired. She broke
both hips. They've never healed properly, so she's
in a wheelchair."

"And the Burroughs couple?" Jupe questioned.

"Fairly new employees. Mrs. Chumley hired them in February. That's all. That's the household. There are gardeners, but they come in twice a week. Same for the pool man. Gerhart Malz comes across the road quite often to play chess with Mrs. Chumley, but I can't imagine that he's a threat. Someone is plaguing Letitia Radford, and I don't know why. She blames me, and if she succeeds in having me thrown off this property—well, she might be sorry."

"Sorry, Dr. Woolley?" said Jupe. "Just what do you mean by that?"

"I mean that I don't know too much about the ants here. Are they a new subspecies? Are they a strain of mutants? One thing is certain. They *are* army ants, and army ants will eat anything living.

"The colonies here on this hill will eventually divide," Woolley went on. "Young queen ants will leave the home colonies and take worker ants with them to set up new colonies. I want to be here when that happens. I want to see how many new colonies there will be and how large they will grow—and how fast. How far will they migrate eventually? You haven't seen a migration of army ants, but can you picture a stream of ants a yard or more wide, rippling over the ground, devouring everything in their way? Perhaps they will even invade buildings."

"You're . . . you're saying that they're dangerous?" said Pete.

"Possibly," Woolley answered. "These ants have already eaten several small animals—moles and field mice. They are killer ants. I find the little skeletons out on the hill with the ants still swarming on them. When the ants finish, there's nothing left but bones!"

"In other words," said Jupe, "you may have a time bomb here. A time bomb of ants!"

"Precisely," said Woolley.

There was a wordless sound from the open door of the laboratory. The boys looked around.

Letitia Radford stood there. She made an elegant picture in her white linen dress—except that her eyes were wide with terror.

"Horrible!" she said. "That's just horrible! Killer ants right in my home! I can't stand it!"

And she began to cry.

7

A Tale of Terror

"Letitia, have you ever considered just *not* having hysterics for a change?" said Charles Woolley. He helped her to a seat on one of the stools near the lab table and handed her a box of tissues. "Wipe your eyes like a good girl and calm down," he said. "I promise you, nothing awful is going to happen with those ants as long as I'm here to keep an eye on them. Now, these boys are going to try to help us with the scarecrow problem."

The woman took a tissue and dabbed at her eyes. "What do you mean, help *us*?" she demanded. "Who is us? You and me?"

"Certainly. We're the ones being victimized," Woolley pointed out. "The scarecrow keeps popping out of the shadows at you, and it's hit me on the head and stolen a jar of ants. I think we have to do something about it."

Letitia Radford hiccupped. "All right," she said. "But these boys are . . . are just boys!"

"Would you like to go to some ordinary private detective and tell him you are being bothered by a scarecrow?" asked Woolley. "I imagine he'd be glad to take your money—if he were the taking sort—but would he do anything for you?"

"Probably not," Letitia admitted. "He'd think I'm crazy."

"But I *know* you're not crazy, Letitia," said Woolley. "The scarecrow hit me on the head, remember?"

She shuddered. "Scarecrows!" she said. "They're horrible! All dirty and full of spiders!"

"Full of spiders?" said Jupe. "Most people think that scarecrows are full of straw."

"Well, that too, of course," said Letitia Radford. "But spiders live in the straw. You'd know if you'd ever had a scarecrow fall on you. I did when I was little. One Halloween I went with my parents to buy a pumpkin at a farm in the valley. There was a scarecrow on the fence there, just as there is here. I wanted to see what he looked like close up, and I climbed the fence and the scarecrow . . . it . . . it . . ."

"It fell on you?" prompted Jupe.

She nodded. "It was terrible. He was so dirty. He must have been sitting on that fence for a million years. He broke apart when he fell, and there were spiders in him—nests of spiders. They ran across my face and got in my hair. Ugh! I hate to think of it, even today."

"Hmmm," said Jupiter. "So you are extraordinarily afraid of scarecrows—and spiders!"

"I don't like *any* kind of bugs," said Letitia. She looked around with distaste, suddenly aware she was in Woolley's lab.

"I can see why you aren't happy to have me around," said Woolley. "But believe me, I wouldn't do anything to upset you. Why should I, for heaven's sake? What would I have to gain?"

"What would *anyone* have to gain?" asked Letitia. "I'm not in anyone's way. I don't hurt anyone. I'm just trying to live quietly here in the house that's really my home—and I can't! I'm being driven mad by a scarecrow!"

She appeared to be on the point of tears again. Jupiter spoke up quickly. "Miss Radford, let's be logical. Whoever is plaguing you must know that you have a particular aversion to scarecrows. How many people know this?"

Letitia fingered one of her gold earrings and thought a moment. "It isn't a great secret," she said. "Any number of people could know. Mrs. Chumley knows, of course. She was with us the day that . . . that thing fell on me. She saw the spiders. But thinking Mrs. Chumley is the scarecrow is silly! She's always been kind to me. And even if she wanted to scare me, she couldn't. She hasn't left that wheelchair for five years except to go to bed. And then she has to be helped."

"How about Burroughs and his wife?" asked Jupiter. "Did they know before the harassment began?"

"I . . . I guess they could have. Right after I arrived home, I was watching TV in the living room with Mrs. Chumley, and *The Wizard of Oz* came on. I had to switch channels. I can't bear to watch that movie even though the scarecrow is Ray Bolger. I remember Burroughs was there when the picture came on. I said something to Mrs. Chumley about how I still didn't like scarecrows. She may have said something to Burroughs later about what had happened when I was a child."

"She told me," said Woolley. "She said she thought it was a shame that you were still upset by *The Wizard of Oz*."

"Gerhart Malz was there that day, too," added Letitia. "I remember now. He comes to visit Mrs. Chumley pretty often, so he could know about my fear, too."

"And all of this took place before you saw the scarecrow for the first time?" asked Jupe.

"Yes. It was the first week I was home. I was just trying to relax and not worry about too many things. I'd had some trouble in Europe."

She stopped, and Jupe thought of the broken engagement. He wondered how old Letitia Radford was. There were lines around her mouth, and a weariness in her eyes. She was no longer young, and she seemed chronically unhappy.

"It was a few days after the TV show that I got into the car one evening to go for a drive down along the coast," she went on. "He . . . it . . . was in the back seat. It gave a horrid sort of gurgling laugh and stood up. I've got a convertible, so it could move without any trouble. It flung out its arms and . . . and all of a sudden there were bugs in my hair and on my lap. Not ants. You know those nasty bugs that you find when you turn over rocks? They're black and they're about an inch long and they're hinged like little armored tanks.

"I screamed, and the scarecrow jumped out of the car. And by the time Burroughs and his wife ran out onto the porch, it was gone!"

"Gee, that's an awful thing to happen!" exclaimed Pete.

"Yes, it was."

"So the scarecrow obviously knew about your twin fears," said Jupe. "He could have learned about it from anyone in your household or perhaps from Gerhard Malz. Tell me about Mr. Malz."

Letitia shrugged. "There isn't much to tell. He's been curator of the Mosby collection for ages. He was at the Mosby place before old Mr. Mosby died, and now he lives in the Mosby house and . . . and that's all I can think of."

"That isn't a lot," said Bob, who had been making notes.

Jupe looked appealingly at Woolley, who shook his head. "Don't ask me," he said. "I haven't paid that much attention to the man."

Letitia Radford frowned in concentration. "Really," she said, "there isn't a lot to know about Gerry.

He went to the Graham Art Institute in Los Angeles, and then he went to work for Mr. Mosby. He lives in the Mosby house and he superintends the men who work there during the day. He does restoration work on the paintings and other things in the collection, and he shows visitors around the galleries. They have to make appointments before they can come, so he can see to it that he's not overworked. I think he's got a nice job."

"Does he have any family?" Jupe asked.

"No," said Letitia. "I've never heard him talk about anyone."

"A loner, eh?" said Jupe. "What does he do with his spare time?"

"Nothing much. He plays chess with Mrs. Chumley, and that's about all." She brightened. "Come to think of it, he's coming to lunch today and then he and Mrs. Chumley are going to play chess. Want to meet him? You can come to lunch, too."

Jupiter nodded. "Thank you. We *would* like to meet him. I think we should get to know everyone whom you see regularly. Because the person who's persecuting you is most likely someone you know!"

8

The Treasure Vault

Lunch was served in the dining room of the Radford mansion, with Mrs. Chumley sitting at the head of the long table and Letitia Radford at the foot. Gerhart Malz sat at Mrs. Chumley's right, and talked at length about the Mosby Museum.

"We have a really first-rate Vermeer," he told the boys. He had lively blue eyes behind gold-rimmed spectacles, and his close-cropped hair was so fair that it was almost white. There was a ruddy tint to his skin, and veins showed in his cheeks and across the bridge of his nose. "Vermeer is a marvel," he went on. "One of the greatest of the Dutch painters. Mrs. Chumley is devoted to him. Aren't you, Mrs. Chumley?"

The woman at the head of the table nodded.

"Mrs. Chumley has a copy of our Vermeer," said Malz. "It's called 'Woman with a Rose,' and it was done by a student. We let people who want to study the techniques of the old masters come into the galleries and copy the famous pictures. They have to get permission in advance, of course, and the copies can't be the same size as the original."

"My copy of the Vermeer is larger than the real one," said Mrs. Chumley. "If it weren't for that, you couldn't tell which is which."

She had finished her lunch, and she put her napkin down on the table. "Would you boys care to see my picture?" she asked.

Malz didn't wait for an answer. He wheeled Mrs. Chumley away from the table. Letitia and the boys followed him across the hall to a little sitting room that had windows looking out over the lawns behind the house. Through an open door the boys could see that the sitting room was part of a suite; a bedroom adjoined it.

"These were my mother's rooms," said Letitia. "I've always liked it here. It's cozy in the winter when the fire is lighted."

"Now, dear, you know I don't have to stay here," said Mrs. Chumley. "There's a spare bedroom in the servants' wing. I can move my things there."

"Don't be silly, Mrs. Chumley," said Letitia. "There's no reason for you to leave here."

She pointed to the picture that hung over the mantel. "There's the copy of the Vermeer," she said.

The boys looked in silence. The painting was a life-size study of a young woman in a blue dress and a lace cap. She stood looking out of a window, holding a yellow rose in her hand.

"Lovely, isn't it?" said Malz.

Mrs. Chumley swung her wheelchair about. "You don't expect any visitors at the museum this afternoon," she said to Malz. "Why don't you take the boys across the road and show them the original—and give them one of your special tours?"

"I would be delighted," said Malz, "but we have a date to play chess, remember?"

"We can play later," said Mrs. Chumley.

"Very well," said Malz. "Would you boys care to see the treasures?"

"Sure!" said Jupiter. "My uncle and aunt were here some years ago when Mr. Mosby was still alive. My aunt still talks about it."

Malz glanced at Letitia Radford. "Want to come?" he asked.

"Thanks, but no thanks," she said. "I've seen the Mosby place at least a million times."

"Then we'll be back in a little while," said Malz, ignoring Letitia's rudeness. He led the boys across the road to the windowless building that housed the Mosby collection of fine art.

"There are a great many bank vaults that aren't as secure as this house," said Malz. He rang the doorbell and a guard let them in. Inside was a square entrance hall, empty except for several display cases and an ancient tapestry which showed a maiden reading in a field filled with flowers.

"Every aspect of this building contributes to the safety of the artworks," said Malz. "You've seen that there are no windows. The alarm system was specially designed for the building. We have guards in the daytime only because visitors come then. The lighting duplicates the daylight, but it's arranged so as to cast no shadows, and it carries no heat to fade or crack old surfaces, as sunlight does. The humidity here is controlled, and the temperature remains the same twenty-four hours a day. The place is a curator's dream."

Malz began to show the boys through the strange building. Downstairs they saw rooms paneled with wood taken from European castles. There were cases filled with antique silver and rare old glass and beautiful illuminated books.

"But what about the famous paintings?" said Jupiter at last.

"Upstairs," Gerhart Malz told him. He led the boys up a staircase that turned and twisted next to an oddly angled wall. There were two broad landings on the stairs, and on one stood a huge grandfather clock ticking away.

Marble-topped tables stood against the walls of the upper hall. On each was some curious and lovely thing. "Wait and see this," said Malz. He stopped beside one of the tables. "It's almost two. Now watch the crystal prisms hanging on this candelabra."

The boys stared at the large silver candelabra on

the table. The clock on the staircase chimed the hour—and the prisms on the candelabra quivered.

"I enjoy that," said Gerhart Malz. "The prisms are so delicately balanced that they vibrate when the old clock strikes. They're in tune with that clock. The candelabra is a new acquisition. I bought it last year. With the approval of the board of directors, of course."

He walked on, and the boys followed him into a room that contained a small desk made of some light-colored wood, a delicately crafted chair, and one painting.

"Gosh!" said Pete.

The painting was the original of the one they had seen hanging in Mrs. Chumley's sitting room.

"It's the same, and yet it's different," said Bob as he studied the portrait of the woman with a rose.

"The difference, of course, is that this one was painted by Vermeer," said Malz. "The copy is excellent—but only a copy. It lacks the master's touch."

The boys were silent for a few minutes. Then Bob said, in a puzzled tone, "It looks so new. Didn't Vermeer live a long time ago?"

"More than three hundred years ago," said Malz. "This painting was probably done about 1660. When Mr. Mosby bought it, it had several old coats of varnish on it and it looked quite brown. I removed the varnish, and there was that fresh, lovely color."

"Was it hard to do that?" asked Pete.

"To clean a picture is an art in itself," said Malz. "It's rewarding, though. We have several Rembrandts in the next room that used to be all dull browns and yellows, with deep black shadows. But Rembrandt didn't paint that way. I worked on the pictures and now they're colorful and vibrant and full of life. Come. I'll show you!"

As they went into the hall, Jupiter sniffed the air. "There's an oily smell," he said. "Is that from something you use in your work?"

"You're getting a whiff of oil paint or perhaps one of the solvents I use on the pictures," said Malz. "My workshop's on the third floor. That's not open to visitors—even very special ones like you boys. The third floor is also where I live."

Bob looked around. "I should think it would get lonely here. It's awfully quiet."

"Sometimes it *is* lonesome," said Malz. "I keep an apartment in Santa Monica, and I go there when I get tired of the quiet here. But on the whole I enjoy my own company as much as anyone's."

Malz moved briskly on to a gallery next to the Vermeer room, and there the boys saw the Rembrandts that he had restored—a landscape and a portrait of an old woman. They went on from one room to another. There were paintings by Reubens and Van Dyke and other great masters—and many by artists who were not quite so well known.

It was more than half an hour before Malz

announced that the tour was over. He ushered the boys down the stairs and out the front door. The guard was no longer in the front hall, so Malz locked the heavy door behind him. Next, with a second key he activated the alarm system. Then he and the boys started across the road toward the Radford house.

They were halfway across when the screaming began. It shattered the peace of the summer afternoon. Shrill and piercing, it went on and on.

"Not again!" exclaimed Pete, and he began to run.

9

The Mysterious Watcher

Pete and Bob cut across the lawn and dashed up the brick steps to the terrace.

"It's Letitia again," said Malz in a weary voice as he and Jupiter followed more slowly.

Letitia Radford stood beside the pool, barefoot and in a wet bathing suit. She clutched a big towel and she screamed.

"Letitia, stop that!" cried Mrs. Chumley.

Jupe stared. So far as he could see, there was absolutely nothing the matter. Yet Letitia Radford continued to scream.

Mrs. Burroughs came striding from the house. She took Letitia by the shoulders and gave her a good shake.

Letitia stopped screaming and began to cry. Mrs. Burroughs put her arms around her. "There now, miss," she said. "There now. It's all right."

Mrs. Burroughs coaxed Letitia into the mansion. The boys heard the housekeeper saying soothing things as she and Letitia went up the stairs.

"What happened?" said Gerhart Malz.

Before Mrs. Chumley could answer, Charles Woolley appeared on the brick steps leading up from the lawn. "I heard screams—for a change," he said.

Burroughs came out onto the terrace looking cool and undisturbed. "I have disposed of the animal," he announced.

Charles Woolley scowled. "Animal? What animal?"

Mrs. Chumley sighed. "Letitia went for a swim," she said, "and when she got out of the pool a great big hairy spider came scuttling across the terrace. It ran right over her bare foot. Of course she screamed!"

"I believe it was the spider called the tarantula," said Burroughs. "I succeeded in capturing it by throwing a towel over it. It is now in the trash barrel—quite dead. I took the liberty of throwing the towel away along with the creature."

"Of course, Burroughs," said Mrs. Chumley. "You did quite right."

"A tarantula!" said Woolley. "I can't blame Letitia for getting upset. I wouldn't enjoy having a tarantula run across my bare foot, and I *like* spiders."

"She'll be sure it's part of a plot," said Malz. "She thinks everything is part of a plot."

Mrs. Chumley looked weary. "It isn't good for her to spend so much time here doing nothing," she said. "I wish she'd go back to Europe. Or at least get out of this house for a while. I think that as soon as she's calmer, I'll suggest that she go into Beverly Hills and stay for a few days. She could get in touch with some of her old friends and do some shopping, and of course see Dr. Wimple. I think I'd better call Dr. Wimple. He should know about this latest scare."

"He will," predicted Malz. "Letitia will not fail to inform her psychiatrist that a tarantula has joined the cast of things that torture her."

"You speak as if she imagined these things," said Jupe. "The tarantula isn't imaginary. It couldn't be. Burroughs just killed it and put it in the trash."

"Oh, of course it isn't imaginary. I didn't mean it that way," said Malz quickly. "But it isn't part of a plot, either. It's just a coincidence that it appeared on the terrace today."

"I suppose so," said Jupiter.

Malz stared at Jupe. "You sound as if there really could be something to Letitia's whims and fancies."

"Perhaps there is," said Jupe. He looked at his watch. "After three. We'd better get started back to Rocky Beach."

"Come back again," invited Mrs. Chumley.

"Thank you," said Jupiter. "And please give our thanks to Miss Radford for the lunch."

"I'll be in touch," promised Charles Woolley, and he waved the boys on their way.

"A curious household," said Jupiter as The Three Investigators made their way downhill to the barn, where they had left their bicycles. "The only one who seems like an intruder there is Letitia Radford, and it's her home. The others behave as if she's a naughty child who came in where she wasn't wanted. Even when she obviously is not imagining things—and she did not imagine a tarantula or a walking scarecrow—the others act as if she's a little girl seeing a bogeyman."

"Maybe she asks for it," said Pete. "How many times has she had hysterics since we met her?"

"True," said Jupe. "She is not a calm person."

"Do you think that tarantula was planted, like the ants were?" asked Bob.

"Maybe, maybe not." Jupe shrugged. "Tarantulas aren't unknown in this area. But the spider certainly fits into the pattern of harassment."

He suddenly stood still in the path and listened. There was a rustling noise off to his left.

"Someone is in the cornfield!" said Jupe softly.

"Let's go!" said Pete, and he started to sprint toward the field.

The rustling became the crash of someone racing away, trampling the corn as he went. The boys dashed after the intruder, but they were only halfway through the field when they heard a car start on the lane below the Radford place. They broke through into the clear just as a nondescript old truck went roaring up the road toward Chaparral Canyon.

"Darn!" cried Pete.

Bob stared after the truck, trying to make out the license number, but the vehicle was moving too fast and raising too much dust.

"The plot thickens!" cried Jupe. He came panting up to his companions, his face red with exertion but glowing with excitement.

"This adds a new dimension to our puzzle," he declared. "I was ready to conclude that one of the people in the Radford house was responsible for the persecution of Letitia Radford. Now it seems that someone, who is not part of the household is interested in what goes on there."

"You think we just chased the scarecrow?" asked Bob.

"I don't know," Jupiter replied. "But the intruder's behavior is suspicious. Why should he flee from us?"

"It could have been just some kid poking around," said Pete.

"Unlikely," said Jupiter. "The person had a car."

Jupe looked over at the old boarded-up house that stood next to the Radford property. The front yard of the ancient place was a tangle of weeds, and the For Sale sign by the rutted driveway was faded.

"Doubtless the truck was parked there," said Jupe, pointing to the drive of the abandoned house. "There isn't room on the road to park a truck and leave it."

He climbed the fence out of the cornfield and trudged toward the house. The other boys followed.

As Jupe had guessed, there was a fresh oil stain in the sloping driveway of the ruined place. Jupe looked up toward the Radford house. He was far enough to the side of it so that the eucalyptus trees on the hill no longer blocked the entire view of the mansion. But now the barn was partly in the way.

"If I were spying on the Radford house," said Jupiter, "I would either get closer, as our unknown intruder just did, or I would climb higher."

Bob pointed to the unboarded upper windows of the old house. "Up there?"

"Of course," said Jupiter.

The boys searched then, and soon found the back door that was unlocked. They crept into the house, through the dim, empty rooms on the first floor, and then up the creaking stairs.

A sudden skittering sound made the boys freeze. "Mice!" said Pete. He relaxed and clomped loudly up the rest of the stairs, as if to scare off anything else in the house.

In the back of the house on the second floor there was a room that had wide windows with no glass.

"You get a great view of the Radford place from here," said Pete. "You can see the back windows and some side windows and part of the terrace and the lawns. And that's just what someone's been seeing." Pete pointed to the floor, where several cigarette butts had been ground out on the bare boards.

"A mysterious watcher," said Jupe. "Did he see Letitia Radford react to the tarantula just now, and then start toward the Radford place? Or was he up at the Radford house when the tarantula appeared? We have no way of knowing, do we?"

Jupe's manner was cheerful, as it often was when a case took an unusual turn. "At this point we have a number of suspects who might be capable of frightening Letitia Radford."

"And knocking Woolley cold, too," said Pete. "Let's not forget Woolley. He's our client."

"Yes, he did engage us," agreed Jupiter. "And let's not forget him. Because he's a suspect, too. After all, what do we know of him? Simply what he's told us. Is he really an entomologist? Or does he have some other reason for wanting to be on the Radford estate?"

"What other reason could he have?" demanded Pete.

"We don't know. What reason would anyone have for tormenting Letitia Radford? Does she threaten someone? Has she injured someone?

"I suggest we find out more about our suspects. Mrs. Chumley cannot possibly be the scarecrow, since she cannot walk. But let's check into Burroughs and his wife. And Malz. He doesn't seem the type to steal insects, but nothing is impossible. And Woolley. He's the one who put up the scarecrow on the fence, and who has unwittingly provided the ants that were put on Letitia Radford's bed. Perhaps he knows more than he lets on. Or perhaps the attacks on Letitia are an attempt to get at Woolley.

"We have to find a motive for the strange happenings here. When we know more about the people involved, we may have a motive. We can get started on our research first thing tomorrow!"

10

Seaching for Answers

At ten the next morning Pete Crenshaw presented himself at the reference desk of the research library at U.C.L.A. Dr. Barrister, a professor at Ruxton University, had called the library on his behalf. Barrister had been involved in one of the cases that The Three Investigators had solved, and had become a fast friend of the boys'. He often advised them when they needed information on academic subjects.

The girl at the desk was not a great deal older than Pete. She grinned when he introduced himself and mentioned Dr. Barrister's telephone call.

"So you're the one who's doing a paper on ants," she said. She took two books off a shelf behind the desk. "These are the books Dr. Woolley wrote about his work in Panama. They're the ones you wanted, aren't they?"

"Yep," said Pete, hoping they were. He felt

uncomfortable posing as a serious student. Suppose someone asked him a question he couldn't answer? Pete was an athlete, not a book lover. But Jupe had dismissed his objections to this library assignment, saying that a good detective had to be at home in many worlds. He had helped Pete work out a cover story and told him to relax.

Pete carried Dr. Woolley's books to a long table that was flanked by brightly colored chairs. He sat down, opened one of the books, and began to read.

Half an hour later he pushed the books aside. He understood very little more about army ants than he had when he first entered the library. The books were extremely technical, and were filled with mysterious scientific terms. However, they were comparatively new and they still had their dust jackets. On each dust jacket was a photograph of Charles Woolley and a brief biography of the entomologist.

Pete made notes on a small pad he had brought with him. Charles Woolley had earned his bachelor's degree at U.C.L.A. and his master's at Stanford, and had returned to U.C.L.A. for his doctor's degree in entomology. His expedition to Panama had taken place three years before. In addition to his degrees and his expedition, the book jackets noted that Charles Woolley was unmarried, and that he was an assistant professor at U.C.L.A.

Pete carried the books back to the reference desk.

"Find out what you needed to know?" said the girl who had helped him.

"I sure did," said Pete, bravely.

"I'll bet," said the girl. "I took one of Dr. Woolley's courses once, and what he doesn't know about ants isn't worth knowing. I thought it was going to be an easy way to get three credits in science. Was I ever wrong! The human bug really put us through the wringer."

"The human bug?" Pete echoed. "Is that what his students call him?"

She laughed and then suddenly looked serious. "Maybe I shouldn't have said that. Is he a friend of yours?"

"Not exactly," said Pete. "I met him a while ago up in the mountains. The Santa Monica Mountains, I mean. He's doing some research there. And he does look kind of like a bug!"

"Right," said the girl. "Also he doesn't mix with people if he can help it. Only ants. I'm surprised he even talked to you."

"He told me a little about his work," said Pete, launching into his cover story. "I thought it sounded interesting, and I had to do a biology project this summer, so I decided to study army ants. Did you know there are army ants right here in California?"

"I think I did know," said the girl. "Makes it nice for Dr. Woolley, doesn't it? He doesn't have to keep running off to Panama."

Pete waited for a moment to see if the girl would

have anything further to say about Charles Woolley.
She didn't. She put the books he had given her on
a shelf and went back to a notebook she was studying.

Pete wandered out into the sunlight with his own
notes in his pocket. He was pleased with his
performance, but at the same time he felt oddly let
down. He had discovered nothing new about
Charles Woolley, except that the man was certainly
no impostor. He was Dr. Woolley, an assistant
professor at U.C.L.A. He had indeed written two
books about army ants and had his picture on the
jackets to prove it.

While Pete considered this, Jupiter Jones was
hurrying down Doheny Drive in Beverly Hills. He
had called Letitia Radford that morning and had
asked her which employment agency Mrs. Chumley used when she engaged new help. "The
Barker-Phillips Agency, I guess," Letitia had answered. "They're pretty reliable and my mother
liked them. I imagine Mrs. Chumley calls them
when she wants someone. Shall I ask her?"

"Please don't," said Jupiter. "Don't say anything
to her about this inquiry."

Jupe had then dressed himself in his best slacks
and jacket and taken the bus into Beverly Hills.

The Barker-Phillips Agency did business in a
tastefully furnished pair of rooms on the second
floor of a small business building on Doheny. In the
outer office sat a woman with blue-white hair and

fine pink skin. "Yes?" she said, when Jupiter came in.

"My name is Jupiter Jones," said Jupe. "I'm looking for work, and . . ."

"Oh, dear!" said the woman.

"Yes, I know that I'm young," said Jupe quickly. "However, I am intelligent and I am willing to work hard. I could be very useful in a large household. I can clean things and repair things, and if there's a dog to be walked . . ."

The woman laughed. "It's nice to find so much talent in a boy your age," she said. "However, people who have large households usually hire adult servants. Why don't you get a newspaper route? Or apply at one of the markets and see if there's an opening for a box boy."

Jupiter allowed his face to take on a look of great woe. "I had hoped to do better," he said. "Burroughs told me you're very good."

"Burroughs?" said the woman.

"The houseman at the Radford estate," said Jupe.

The woman swung around in her chair, opened the drawer of a filing cabinet, and took out a folder. She looked at it and smiled. "Ah, yes. Burroughs. Lord Armiston's man. Yes. We did place him and his wife with Mrs. Chumley. An excellent man."

"I have references," said Jupe eagerly. "Burroughs told me you check references."

"Certainly we check references," said the woman. "We wouldn't stay in this business very long if the people we recommended weren't reliable. In Burroughs' case, for example, we wired to England to his previous employer. When Lord Armiston assured us by return cable that Burroughs is capable and his wife is an excellent cook, we placed them right away.

"In your case, however, references won't help. We simply don't have positions for young boys."

"I see," said Jupiter.

"I'm surprised that Burroughs would even suggest that you come here," said the woman.

"He didn't exactly suggest it," admitted Jupe. "I thought of it myself when he told me that you'd placed him."

"That's a little different, isn't it?" said the woman. "Well, come back and see us in a few years. Perhaps then we'll have something to talk about."

Jupiter thanked her and went out, frowning furiously. Burroughs was a houseman who had once been employed by a British lord. It did not seem likely that he could be a scarecrow who put ants into people's beds.

While Jupe was boarding the westbound bus, headed for Rocky Beach, Bob was busy farther east. He had ridden in with Jupe, and then had stayed on the bus until it stopped in front of the big, square building that housed the Graham Art Institute. Bob knew a little bit about the school, which had trained many really fine artists. He went up the broad front steps of the place and pulled open a heavy bronze door.

When he stepped through the door, Bob found

himself in a long, wide hall that had doors opening off to either side. The odor in the air reminded him of the Mosby house. It was the smell of oil paints.

"You looking for something, buddy?" said a young man in blue jeans. He had come out of one of the rooms carrying a small stepladder.

"I'm . . . I'm looking for my cousin," said Bob in a hesitant way. Then he frowned. Jupiter would not have stammered or hesitated. Jupiter would have been firm and assured.

Bob took a deep breath and squared his shoulders. "My cousin used to be a student here," he said. "I don't know his present address, and I thought that the school might have a record of his whereabouts."

There! That sounded much better!

"Oh, sure!" said the young man. "They try to keep track of all the alumni. The administration offices are on the second floor in the front of the building. Ask anybody there."

Bob thanked the young man, climbed the stairs at the end of the hall, and found the administration offices. They were a series of glass-enclosed cubicles, and they were empty except for a bearded man who was looking through a card file.

"Yes?" said the man when he saw Bob. "You wanted something?"

"My cousin used to be a student here," said Bob. "His name is Gerhart Malz. I'm visiting in Los Angeles, and my mother told me to call him while

I'm here, but I can't find his name in the telephone book."

"Malz?" said the man. "Why, sure. He was a student of mine, a long time ago. He's the curator now at the Mosby Museum."

Bob allowed his face to remain blank, as if he had never heard of the Mosby Museum. The bearded man turned away from the card file. "The Mosby Museum is way out in the hills above Rocky Beach," he said, "so don't try to get there on your own. The museum's listed in the telephone book. Call your cousin. I understand Gerry's as proud of that museum as if he owned it. Let him come and get you and show you through the place. I hope you like old masters."

"You mean pictures?" said Bob.

"Right. Pictures by artists like Rembrandt and Van Dyke and Vermeer. The Mosby house is full of them."

"Oh," said Bob. "Well . . . uh . . . I suppose that'll be interesting. A curator's a pretty important person, isn't he? I mean . . . I guess my mother will be glad to know Gerry's doing some important work."

A rather bleak look came over the face of the bearded man. "Your cousin has a very good, secure position," he said. "If that's what would please your mother, she's bound to be pleased."

"Well, it sounds better than *not* having a good job," said Bob.

"It depends," said the man, and there was an edge to his voice. "Artists look at things differently sometimes."

"How differently?"

"Well, some of us think that a guy with Gerry's talent ought to be doing his own paintings instead of looking after the ones somebody else has already finished," said the man. "You can tell him I said so. My name's Edward Anson. Not that your cousin will care. He's heard all this before, but when I think of that talent going to waste . . . well, I just get furious."

"You really want me to tell him that?" said Bob. "I . . . I don't know him, you know. I mean we never met. He's my mother's second cousin and we're not a close family. He might not like it. Maybe he won't like me showing up. Is he . . . well . . . friendly?"

"I'm sorry," said the man. "I didn't mean to unload on you. I suppose Gerry's friendly enough for most ordinary purposes. He does the right thing, you can count on that. Probably he'll take a day off and take you to Disneyland or Magic Mountain. That's not very original. But then he wasn't always very original. He was a tremendous mimic. He could duplicate the style of just about any painter, did you know that?"

The man paused, then said, "Of course you didn't know that. You don't even know Gerry, do you? Don't pay any attention to me. I'm just a crusty old idealist who believes it's good for young artists to be hungry instead of secure. Stirs up the creative juices." The man smiled. "Go and call Gerry, and when you see him, tell him to come and see me sometime."

"Yes, sir," said Bob.

He was turning away when the man said, "A cousin. Funny. Never knew that Gerry had any family. He never talked about anybody. He always seemed so self-sufficient and . . . and buttoned up."

Bob smiled. "Everybody has some family," he pointed out.

"Very true," said the teacher. "We don't get human beings from a people factory yet, do we? It's just that sometimes it's hard to think of people in relation to mothers and fathers. You go and call Gerry and have a good time in Los Angeles. And remember, tell Gerry to come and see me. I'd like to talk to him about his work."

"Yes, sir," said Bob. "Thanks very much."

Bob went down the stairs and out through the big front door. There was a bus coming along and he ran to catch it. He settled next to a window for the long ride out to the coast, and pondered on the interview he had just had. He had learned that Malz had talent, that he was considered self-sufficient and "buttoned up," and perhaps more devoted to security than to art. These facts added to the picture of Malz but didn't change it. He was, without doubt, exactly what he appeared to be—a capable curator.

Bob sighed. His investigation had turned up nothing suspicious. He wondered if Jupe or Pete had had better luck. If not, the detectives would have to try a new approach. One way or another, they would identify that scarecrow!

11

The Scarecrow Strikes!

"What do you mean, you looked me up?" demanded Charles Woolley. "How dare you? I've told you everything you need to know about me!"

"We have found it best not to take people too much on faith, Dr. Woolley," said Jupiter. "We have investigated everyone we can think of who might be connected with the harassment of Letitia Radford."

It was just dusk. Jupiter, Pete, and Bob had spent the afternoon doing chores and comparing notes. After supper they had ridden out to the Radford estate to talk with their client. They had found Woolley in his laboratory, and he had reacted with rage when Pete mentioned his trip to U.C.L.A.

"I understand how you feel, Dr. Woolley," said Jupiter now, "but you must agree that it is our business to doubt—and to satisfy our doubts.

"So far as we can tell, no one in the Radford

77

household has any motive for this campaign of terror against Letitia Radford, so we must look elsewhere. There is no apparent point to this cruelty, and yet someone is going to great lengths to be cruel."

Woolley sighed. "She isn't a clever woman and she can be rude and irritating," he said. "But I can't imagine that she's ever willingly hurt anyone."

"Could she have hurt someone without intending to?" Jupe asked. "You said once that she had been engaged to marry a number of times, and that no marriage ever took place. Perhaps she jilted someone."

"According to Mrs. Chumley, Letitia doesn't jilt people," said Woolley. "She's the one who gets jilted."

"Oh?" said Jupiter.

"Yes. Mrs. Chumley has also hinted that some of her fiancés were unsuitable and that Letitia's brother paid them to get lost. Some were adventurers of the worst kind, only out for her money and willing to be bought off. And I guess some simply got fed up with her. She's hard to be with for any length of time."

Jupe nodded. "Where is she now?"

"In Beverly Hills at the moment, but she won't be there long," said Woolley. "She calmed down last night and decided that the spider that ran over her foot didn't do it on purpose. Mrs. Chumley persuaded her to go into Beverly Hills for a few days and enjoy herself.

"I went up to the big house this afternoon to borrow some coffee, and Mrs. Burroughs told me Letitia had bumped into an old boyfriend in the Beverly Wilshire Hotel. It upset her so much that she called and said she's coming home tonight.

"Mrs. Chumley tried to persuade her to move to another hotel and forget it, but she wouldn't. She's coming back here."

Hardly were the words out of Woolley's mouth when the boys heard a scream.

"She's arrived!" said Pete, and he started for the door.

Jupe and Bob were close behind him as he ran up the hill. Charles Woolley followed, muttering angrily.

It was almost dark now. The screaming went on. Letitia Radford sounded more terrified than they had ever heard her.

"No!" she shrieked. "No! Don't! Please don't!"

The shrieks broke off, and there was violent weeping. And then, bearing down on the boys like some fearful hobgoblin, came the scarecrow!

The terrace lights went on above them and they caught a glimpse of the scarecrow's grinning face—a face made of coarse material that puckered around the neck where it was gathered and tied with a cord. Eyes glittered in black triangles on the face, beneath the brim of a black hat. Just like the scarecrow on the fence, this one wore an old corduroy jacket with straw sticking out of the sleeves. The creature stood still for an instant when it saw Woolley and the boys, and Woolley gasped in horror. The scarecrow carried a scythe!

"Watch out!" shouted Pete.

With a low, gurgling laugh, the scarecrow raised the scythe and made a sweeping motion. Then it charged toward The Three Investigators, and the hideous weapon in its gloved hands swung up!

"Oh, no!" breathed Bob. He threw himself aside, out of the way of the deadly curved blade.

Jupe tried to run, but he stumbled and fell, hands clutching at his head and body doubled over to shield himself from the fiend's attack.

Pete stood as if paralyzed. The handle of the scythe connected with his forehead. An instant later he was stretched on the ground, and the scarecrow was crashing away down the hill. Woolley jumped to get out of its way.

The boys heard the thing dash through the eucalyptus grove. Then there was silence.

"Pete!" said Bob. "Pete, are you okay?"

Pete sat up slowly and rubbed his head. "Yeah. It didn't hit me hard. I just . . . just couldn't seem to get out of the way."

"You might have been killed by that thing!" exclaimed Woolley.

"Listen!" Jupe looked toward the top of the hill.

Letitia Radford was making a low, whimpering sound, like a small animal that has been injured. There were lights on in front of the Radford house, and the boys could hear Burroughs and Mrs.

Chumley. They both seemed to be trying to comfort Letitia.

The Three Investigators reached the house in time to see Burroughs help Letitia up the steps to the front door. Mrs. Chumley sat in the hall behind Burroughs, looking anxious. Letitia's convertible stood in the driveway. Its door was still open on the driver's side.

"It . . . it had a scythe!" moaned Letitia. "Just like the Grim Reaper! It was going to cut my head off!"

"Oh, surely not, Miss Letitia!" said Burroughs.

"It was! It was!"

Jupiter, Pete, and Bob went up the steps into the hall. "It did have a scythe," said Jupiter. "We saw it."

"Well, now, I've had enough, I have," said Mrs. Burroughs. She came bustling up from the back of the house, breathless and with her cap askew. "All this screeching and rambling about. I've called the police."

"Oh, dear!" said Mrs. Chumley.

"Good!" exclaimed Charles Woolley, who had come in after the boys. "Now maybe that police chief will pay some attention to all this."

"I should hope so," said Mrs. Burroughs. She went to Letitia and led her toward the living room. "Come now, miss. I'll make you a nice cup of tea. Calm your nerves. Must have given you a proper shock, seeing that horrid thing. I looked out the window and saw it myself, with that great, nasty knife thing in its hands."

They heard tires on the road outside. Jupe turned and saw headlights as a car pulled into the drive in front of the Mosby Museum. The headlights went off and a man got out of the car and started across the road. It was Gerhart Malz.

"What's up?" he called. "Anything the matter?"

"It's the scarecrow, sir," said Burroughs, stepping to the doorway. "He was waiting in the driveway when Miss Letitia came home."

"Oh, that!" said Malz in a disgusted tone.

"Don't say 'Oh, that' as if the woman imagined it!" cried Woolley. His bald head gleamed and his eyes snapped. He looked more than ever like a highly intelligent ant. "We all saw it and it's a menace. Somebody could have been killed!"

From far away down the mountainside came the wail of sirens.

"Ah, the police!" said Mrs. Burroughs. "I wasn't sure they'd come. The officer I talked to seemed doubtful about catching a scarecrow!"

"I'll bet Chief Reynolds is with them," said Jupiter in a mournful tone, "and I'll bet he isn't going to be happy to see *us* here!"

12

The Night Watch

The next morning, The Three Investigators met in Headquarters in The Jones Salvage Yard. As Jupiter had predicted, Chief Reynolds had been highly annoyed to find the boys at the Radford estate the previous evening. He brushed aside their objection that he himself had recommended them for the scarecrow case. The chief had earlier told the boys to stay out of trouble, and here they were, once again, in the midst of a dangerous situation. The boys were ordered to go home and forget about the scarecrow.

As Chief Reynolds might have predicted, Jupiter, Pete, and Bob had no intention of abandoning their case. "But we'd better be careful," said Jupe to his companions. "The chief really will make trouble if he sees us at the Radford place again."

"After last night, I'm going to be awfully careful," Pete declared.

"You got the worst of it last night," said Bob,

"except for Letitia. At least now things should be easier for her. Now everybody in the house *knows* there's a scarecrow!"

Jupe nodded. "There are few things more maddening than not being believed. It's enough to drive anyone to a breakdown." The First Investigator sat behind the desk in the tiny office in Headquarters and pulled at his lip in a manner that indicated he was thinking intensely. "Well, a lot of us saw the scarecrow last night. And that means we can start eliminating suspects. Woolley was with us. Mrs. Burroughs said she saw the scarecrow out the window. Her husband and Mrs. Chumley were right there on the scene. That leaves only Gerhart Malz unaccounted for."

"Gee, he could easily have been the scarecrow," said Bob. "Say he left his car parked on Rock Rim Drive. After scaring Letitia he would have had time to run down there, get rid of his scarecrow outfit, then drive back to the Mosby place before the police arrived."

"It's possible," said Jupiter. "Malz knew of Letitia's fear of scarecrows and insects all along. And he could have learned that she'd be returning early from Beverly Hills.

"But don't forget our mysterious unknown watcher—the person we chased through the cornfield. Perhaps he's been watching the Radford place from the old house on Rock Rim Drive for some time. He just might be the scarecrow. But we have no way of knowing unless we catch him at it."

Pete shuddered. "I'm not anxious to catch *any-body* at it," he declared. "After what happened last night?"

"We'll have to be very careful, but we *must* stalk the scarecrow," said Jupe. "We are the only ones willing to be on the scene. The police aren't that involved yet. And we do know a few things about the scarecrow that could be helpful."

"We know that he's handy with a scythe!" said Pete. "What else do we know?"

"He always appears at dusk," said Jupe. "At least, every time Letitia Radford has seen him, it's been just before dark—that twilight time when it's hard to see clearly."

"I think I see a stakeout coming," said Bob.

"Exactly," said Jupe. "This evening, before dark, we'll go to the Radford house and watch and wait."

"Suppose nothing happens?" said Bob.

"Then we return tomorrow night," said Jupiter.

"Suppose something *does* happen?" Pete said. His voice quavered slightly. "Suppose the scarecrow comes?"

"Then we keep out of sight, watch him, and try to find out where he goes," Jupe decided. "Now here's what I had in mind. We'll take our walkie-talkies so that we can keep in touch with one another. Bob, you watch the Mosby house; Gerhart Malz is a prime suspect now. Pete, you hide near the old house on Rock Rim. I'll patrol the Radford place."

Pete sighed. "All right. I'll go. I won't like it, but I'll go."

Pete was still apprehensive that evening when he and the other two Investigators hid their bikes in a clump of scrub brush about a quarter of a mile from the Radford house. Jupiter handed a walkie-talkie radio to Pete and another to Bob.

The little sending-and-receiving units had been built by Jupe himself in his workshop at the salvage yard. Similar to CB radios, each set consisted of a speaker and a microphone. The Investigators each wore a belt with copper wire sewn to it, and each belt had a lead-in wire that could be plugged into the radio. The belts with the wires acted as antennas for the radios, which could broadcast for half a mile or more. When one of the boys wanted to speak into his microphone, he pressed a button on the set. When he wanted to listen, he released the button.

"Now, if you see the scarecrow, don't try to interfere with him," warned Jupiter after the boys had plugged in their radios. "Just try to keep him in sight. If you need help, use your walkie-talkie."

Pete nodded, and they walked on in the fading light. When they neared the Radford house Pete left the road, cut across the vacant land just before the Radford property, and made his way down through the underbrush on the hillside to the old house on Rock Rim Drive.

There was no traffic on the rutted old road when Pete reached his destination. No car was parked anywhere in sight. The abandoned house looked black and desolate, with brambles and vines creeping up the walls and a tangle of shrubbery crowding around the front steps.

The sun was just setting when Pete found a hiding place in the bushes beside the drive of the old house.

"Number Two," said his walkie-talkie. "Where are you, Number Two?"

It was Jupe's voice.

Pete pressed the button on his radio. "I'm in the bushes near the old house," he said quietly. "There's nothing moving here."

"Good, Two," said Jupe. "Wait and see what happens. Bob, I can't see you."

There was a click on the radio. "I'm behind the Mosby house," said Bob.

"All right," said Jupe. "It's getting darker. Keep alert, and don't use the walkie-talkie unless you have to."

The radio went silent. Pete sat down on the ground and pulled his knees up under his chin. He waited and listened. At first he heard nothing. But then, faintly, he could hear the sound of a car laboring up the grade from the coast.

Pete tensed. Traffic on Chaparral Canyon Road was not unusual. The car might go on over the crest of the mountains and down into the San Fernando Valley on the other side.

Or would it turn off onto Rock Rim Drive?

The sound of the engine changed as the driver shifted down to a lower gear. Pete decided a truck was coming. He heard springs squeak in protest and he saw headlights on the road. The vehicle had turned onto Rock Rim.

The headlights seemed to pierce Pete's hiding place as the truck jounced up into the drive next to the old house. The driver killed the engine and lights, and Pete heard a hand brake protest as it was yanked on.

The truck door opened and a man got out. He went quietly through the shadows to the back of the house. Pete heard the back door open. An instant later a light flickered through the cracks in the boarded windows.

The man from the truck went directly upstairs. Pete heard his footsteps, loud on the bare floors, as he went to the back of the house.

Pete inched along behind the bushes until he could see the upstairs windows at the back—the windows that gave a view of the Radford mansion. At first the windows gaped empty and black. But a minute later a match flared in one of them. Pete caught a glimpse of a face that was work-worn and tanned, with deep lines running from the nose down to the corners of the mouth.

The man lit a cigarette, and Pete saw a halo of white hair framing his face. Then the match went out. Except for the glowing tip of the cigarette, the house was dark.

Trembling inside, Pete crept back toward the truck. He kept low behind the bushes until he was out of the man's line of sight.

What was the man watching? Pete wondered.

The Radford house—but *what* at the mansion? Would something happen there that would be a signal—that would cause the watcher to put on an old corduroy coat, tie a painted burlap sack over his head, and don the black hat of the scarecrow?

Pete thought of calling Jupe on his walkie-talkie but decided not to risk even whispering. Instead he stood up and pulled at the handles on the rear doors of the truck. The doors swung out.

At first it was totally black inside the vehicle, but after a few minutes the blackness did not seem so intense. Pete reached in and touched a net of some sort. It was attached to a metal rim. There were plastic objects—long-handled tools somewhat like rakes—and there was a strong chemical odor.

Pete got into the truck, touching and sniffing. Chlorine. He smelled chlorine. The tools must be those that were used to clean swimming pools. The watcher in the old house was a pool maintenance man!

Pete grinned wryly to himself. The boys had gone to such lengths to investigate Burroughs and his wife, and Gerhart Malz, and even Woolley, who had hired them in the first place. And they had not given a thought to the casual help who might be familiar with the Radford household—the gardeners and the pool men. Perhaps one of them had a reason to dislike Letitia Radford. Perhaps she had been imperious or impatient. Or perhaps the owner of the truck was a man with a twisted mind—a man who enjoyed making other people suffer.

If only he could put his hands on the scarecrow outfit, thought Pete, he would have proof!

But then he froze, his hands gripping the side of the truck. The vehicle was moving!

"Oh, no!" whispered Pete.

Desperately, without even stopping to think, Pete scrambled over the back of the seat and grabbed at the hand brake. It was loose in his hands. He slid down, hanging on to the steering wheel, trying to guide the truck as it rolled downhill faster and faster, backward and out onto Rock Rim Drive. His foot found the brake and he pumped, but the brake pedal went to the floor, and the sharp smell of brake fluid came to Pete's nostrils. One of the cylinders had gone out. There were no brakes!

Pete wondered briefly if he could slow the truck by slipping it into gear. But the maneuver might not work, and the truck was gaining speed every second. It was time to bail out.

Pete pushed the door open. He saw trees flash past in the twilight. Taking a deep breath, he rolled out of the truck.

There was the sky above him and the road beneath him. Then he hit and rolled some more and the truck was gone, crashing and lurching down the grade. Then Pete was off the road and tumbling down an incline into a ditch. His head struck something hard, and the soft blue-green of the evening sky became a huge, many-colored light in his head. Pete lay still, and for a little while he knew nothing more.

13

Jupe Finds Trouble

The moon was coming up as Jupiter made his fourth slow circuit around the Radford house. He paused on a slight rise in the ground behind the mansion. The night was warm, so in spite of the threat of the scarecrow, the drapes had not been drawn. Jupe could look directly into the lighted rooms. He could see Mrs. Burroughs in the kitchen, scrubbing at the sink. In a small sitting room to the left of the kitchen, only a television set was on. Burroughs could be seen in silhouette, slouched in a chair watching a baseball game.

Over to the right, Mrs. Chumley and Gerhart Malz were playing chess in Mrs. Chumley's little sitting room. As Jupiter watched, Malz smiled, said something to Mrs. Chumley, and moved a piece on the board. She made a wry face.

Jupiter concluded that Malz had won the chess game.

The curator stood up and buttoned his sports

jacket, talking all the while. After a minute or two he went out of the room.

Mrs. Chumley sat for a short time and looked up at her copy of the Vermeer painting. Then, as if she had been struck by a sudden idea, she wheeled herself into the corner bedroom adjoining the sitting room and snapped on the lights there. She went to a closet and opened big double doors. Jupe glimpsed rows of clothes hanging on hangers and stacks of boxes on the shelves above the dresses and coats.

Suddenly Mrs. Chumley looked around at the window. It was almost as if she sensed that someone was watching from the dark lawn outside. She went to the windows and drew the drapes, shutting herself away from Jupe's sight.

Jupe chuckled softly to himself and walked on, making a wide sweep around the right corner of the house. Near the corner the ground sloped downward to expose the basement walls. Beneath Mrs. Chumley's bedroom, a cellar door opened onto a path that led to the right and connected with the driveway. Jupe guessed that this door was the entrance used by maintenance men and delivery men.

Jupe continued along the side of the house, past the four-car detached garage and down the driveway. In the front, the driveway forked to the left to curve past the front entrance. Jupe followed the left fork and then cut across the grass to reach the terrace at the far side of the house.

At the back of the terrace, rooms in the servants' wing were again visible. Mrs. Burroughs was still at the kitchen sink and her husband was still watching the ball game. Jupe stole up the terrace steps and positioned himself behind a large potted plant. All along the left side of the terrace, the long windows of the living room were open. Jupe peeked in and saw Letitia Radford sitting on a sofa, a backgammon set on the coffee table in front of her. Charles Woolley was across from her, stiffly intent in a straight chair. His bald head gleamed in the lamplight and he scowled at the backgammon board.

Gerhart Malz came a few steps into the room and Jupe heard him say, "Well, it looks as if you two have buried the hatchet."

"We are united against a common enemy," said Woolley. He did not look up from the backgammon board.

"Good enough," said Malz. "I'll say good night now. I have some things to catch up on before I leave on vacation."

"You're going on vacation?" said Letitia Radford. "My word! What will happen to the Mosby collection while you're gone?"

"The museum will be closed, Letitia," said Malz. "It's closed the last two weeks of August every year. You know that. One of the regular guards is going to stay in the spare room on the third floor while I'm away, just to see that nothing goes wrong."

"I see," said Letitia. "Mrs. Chumley will certainly miss you. When are you leaving?"

"On Friday," said Malz. "I'll see you before
then."

He turned and went out, and Jupe hurried down
the steps from the terrace to the lawn. He went to
the front of the house and watched Malz cross the
road and go into the museum.

In the near dark, Bob appeared from around a
corner of the Mosby place. He waved silently at
Jupe, then ducked back out of sight.

Jupe returned to the terrace. He saw Mrs.
Chumley come into the living room in her wheelchair. She had a big suit box in her lap.

"Letitia, dear," she said, "when you finish your
game, perhaps we could sort out these pictures."

"What pictures are those?" Letitia asked.

"They're pictures of you, dear," said Mrs. Chumley. "I've been meaning to get them in order for
ever so long. I've been snapping pictures of you
ever since you belonged to the Bluebirds. I have
you at every stage. Everything until you started
living abroad so much."

Mrs. Chumley looked thoughtful. "Not that it
isn't lovely to have you here, dear," she said, "but
perhaps you should be in Europe now. Why don't
you go and join your brother? He's cruising in the
Mediterranean now, isn't he? It would be so
pleasant, and you wouldn't have to worry about that

terrible scarecrow. Chester would look after you. He always knows what to do."

"Mrs. Chumley, I make my brother nervous and you know it," said Letitia. "I am not going to let that . . . that monster drive me out of my own home!"

"Of course not, dear," said Mrs. Chumley. She took the lid off the box of photographs and began to look through them.

Jupiter tiptoed off the terrace and resumed his patrol of the grounds. He felt uneasy. There was something about the scene in the living room that disturbed him. There was something wrong. But before he could puzzle out what it might be, he realized that someone was walking in the shadows down under the eucalyptus trees.

Jupe felt his heart give a great jump. The scarecrow! It had to be him! Malz was in the museum and all the occupants of the Radford house were either in the living room or in the servants' quarters.

Jupiter slipped quietly down toward the trees. He heard the snapping of twigs when he got nearer, and the rustle of leaves as the night prowler went in the direction of the barn.

Jupe stepped into the shadows under the trees just as the creature emerged into the open. It was indeed the scarecrow. It stalked boldly toward the barn, without looking back. But when it reached the barn door, it stopped.

Jupe guessed that there must be a stout padlock on the door. After being assaulted once, and after seeing the scarecrow charge down the hill with the scythe, Woolley had taken steps to protect his lab.

The scarecrow made a noise that was like a wordless growl. It was unbelievably eerie to hear the creature there in the darkness. Instinctively, Jupe stepped back.

His foot came down on something that rolled. His ankle twisted and he fell sideways, crashing into a clump of manzanita.

The scarecrow spun around. Jupe saw the creature rush toward him. Jupe threw his hands up to cover his face and flung himself to one side. And then, with a fearful cry, the scarecrow leaped!

14

The Killer Ants

Jupe tensed himself for the blow that was sure to come. The scarecrow's boots struck the ground just next to his head. But then the creature pounded away, crashing through brush and dead leaves, and Jupe was alone.

Alone and unharmed!

Shaking, Jupe got to his knees. He groped for the walkie-talkie, which he had dropped. He found it and pressed the button on the side.

"Pete! Bob!" His voice shook with excitement. "He was here. I saw him! Do you hear me?"

Jupe released the button. There was a click, and he heard Bob's voice.

"Where are you?"

"Down the hill in the eucalyptus grove," said Jupe. "I think the scarecrow went up toward the house."

The radio clicked again. "He sure didn't come this way," said Pete. His voice sounded strange.

"I've been watching a suspect, but mine isn't the scarecrow. Couldn't be. He was in the old house until a minute ago. Then he had to chase his runaway truck. I guess he decided it wasn't his night. He just drove off."

"Did you get his license number?" asked Bob.

"Nope," said Pete. "Sorry. I wasn't feeling too hot."

"Pete, are you hurt?" asked Jupiter.

"No. I'm okay. I had a fall, that's all."

"Well, keep an eye out in case the scarecrow comes your way. And Bob, you watch the big house, will you?"

"What are you going to do?" asked Bob. His voice was tight with apprehension.

"Try and see where the scarecrow could have gone," said Jupiter.

"For gosh sakes, be careful!" warned Pete.

Jupiter was careful. He moved beneath the eucalyptus trees as silently as a shadow, and he tried to imagine that he was the scarecrow. Where would that haunter of the night go if he were startled—if he had to find cover in a hurry?

Jupe listened. There was no sound except the chirping of cicadas. He was at the edge of the grove, and he could see the big house on the hill. The windows that opened onto the terrace were cheerful squares of light. Beyond them, people were busy at ordinary occupations. They were playing backgammon and sorting photographs. But somewhere on the hillside, in the darkness, the scarecrow had gone to ground. Somewhere the mysterious masquerader was hiding.

The cornfield was behind Jupe, and he dismissed it from his mind. The scarecrow had not gone there. It had run toward the clearer ground behind the house. Jupe walked that way, looking to left and to right. There was nothing moving on the back lawn. He skirted the stand of live oaks down the hill from the Radford mansion, and beyond this he saw a small frame cottage. It nestled in a hollow of the land so that it was not easily noticed. Jupe knew that it must be the guest house where Woolley lived.

Jupe stood still and thought. Would the scarecrow dare go into Woolley's quarters? Was it there now, watching, waiting for Jupe to make a move or to go on by? If Jupe did pass the little house, what would the creature do? Attack him? Escape down the hill to Rock Rim Drive? Or had it already found some other shelter on the brush-covered hillside?

Slowly, Jupe moved toward the little house. He stepped cautiously onto the porch, then decided that stealth was of no use. If the scarecrow was in the house, it had already seen Jupe approach.

Jupe rapped on the door as if he had come looking for Woolley. "Dr. Woolley?" he called. "It's me. Jupiter Jones!"

He rapped again. Then he tried the doorknob. His heart gave a lurch. The door was not even closed tightly. The instant he touched the knob it turned. He pushed and the door swung open.

He waited. When nothing stirred in the little house, he spoke aloud. "I'll leave a note for him," he said. He felt at the wall beside the door until he found a light switch. He touched it, and several lamps glowed.

Jupe was standing on the threshold of a snug little living room. The furniture was rustic and there was a stone fireplace. The kitchen was to the right, a little alcove almost enclosed by a counter.

Jupe could see no hiding place here, so he went on to a door at the far side of the room. He found a tiny hallway, a bathroom, and a bedroom with twin beds. There was no one in the stall shower in the bathroom, and there was no one under the beds or in the closet or behind the door. The house was empty.

Satisfied, Jupe turned to go back to the living room. But then he stopped in the hall and he froze. Into his mind came part of Charles Woolley's lecture on army ants.

"Can you picture a stream of ants a yard wide?" Woolley had said. "Imagine them rippling over the ground, devouring everything, even invading buildings!"

Jupiter did not have to imagine it. He was seeing it. A living river of insects poured over the doorsill. Thousands upon thousands of them marched in a steady, horrifying column across the floor and swarmed over the furniture. One chair was already covered with a waving, undulating carpet of ants.

Again Jupe thought of Woolley's description of the ants. "They will eat anything living," Woolley had said.

"That's foolish!" Jupiter declared. He spoke out loud. "These aren't vicious African driver ants!"

But then Jupe remembered that the ants on the hillside were a new strain, perhaps mutants. Even Woolley knew little about them. Jupe had a sudden vision of ants swarming over his body, each taking a tiny bite out of him, eating him alive.

Jupe turned and fled into the bedroom. He rushed to the window and tried to fling it open. It didn't budge. It was stuck fast!

Jupe yanked off a shoe and raised it high, intending to break the glass. But then he stopped. It would do no good. He hadn't noticed before that the windows of the guest house were covered with iron grillework.

He spun around. The head of the merciless column of marching insects had flowed into the hallway just outside the bedroom.

Jupe was trapped!

15

Fire!

The river of ants flowed through the hallway like some thick, viscous liquid.

Jupe pressed the button on his walkie-talkie. "Pete! Bob!" he cried. "Ants! Millions of ants! In the guest house! Quick! Get Woolley!"

The ants poured through the bedroom door.

"Roger!" said Bob's voice on the radio.

"Hurry!" cried Jupe. "I'm trapped!"

He climbed up onto a bed, yanked the bedspread clear of the floor, and piled it in rumpled folds in the middle of the bed.

"Pete! Bob! Hurry!"

The tide of ants had spread. It was nearer now, and Jupe was screaming into the radio.

He stopped. Someone was running outside the house.

"Good heavens!" exclaimed Charles Woolley.

"Jupe!" It was Bob calling out. "Where are you? You okay?"

"In the bedroom!" cried Jupe. "Hurry, will you?"

Jupe heard Mrs. Burroughs exclaiming loudly about nasty little creatures. Burroughs told her to stand aside. Someone banged at the bedroom window.

Jupe left off watching the ants and looked across to see Pete looking in through the bars at him. Bob was beside Pete. He was reaching through the bars, trying to pry the window open.

"It's stuck!" shouted Jupe. "I think it's painted shut!"

Burroughs and Woolley appeared, and Bob and Pete stepped aside to make way for them. Woolley had a rock in his hand. He tossed it between the bars, and the window shattered.

"Here!" Woolley threw a can to Jupiter. It was insect spray. "This will stop any ants it can hit. Use it quick, and get to the window."

"There's a latch beside the window," said Burroughs. "It will disengage the grille and you can get out."

The first of the ants were crawling up the legs of the bed now, but the floor wasn't completely covered with the insects. Jupe sprayed furiously, aiming the insecticide at the floor next to the bed. He stepped down and ants crunched under his feet. He shuddered, but kept working. Spray, take a step, spray, take another step.

Then he was walking on broken glass.

"The latch?" He looked wildly along the wall. "Where's the latch?"

Burroughs pointed. "Pull the little chest of drawers away from the wall and you'll see it."

Jupe yanked at the small chest. It slid out, crushing ants as it came.

The latch was simple. A piece of steel came in through the wall—an extension of the grillework outside. It had a hole in it, and through this hole a bolt was inserted to hold it in place.

Jupe pulled at the bolt and it came free.

"Got it!" he cried.

"Good boy!" said Woolley. He and Burroughs pulled the grillework away from the window.

A second later Jupiter was out on the grass. Mrs. Burroughs started clucking over him like a mother hen. Charles Woolley stood at the window and stared with fascination at the ants. They now almost covered the bed where Jupe had been stranded.

And then Letitia Radford came running down from the big house. In the lights that shone from the guest cottage, Jupe could see her face. It was convulsed with horror. She had a can in her hand—a red, square can that she carried by a handle on the top.

Jupe blinked, and suddenly he knew what she intended to do.

"Miss Radford, no!" he shouted.

"Keep back!" she cried. "Don't you come near me!"

There was a murderous edge to her voice. She had the top off the can now, and she made a move as if she would hurl the contents at Jupe.

"Letitia! Don't!" begged Woolley. "My ants—my research! Please!"

Letitia Radford looked at Woolley with great scorn. Then she began to slosh liquid from the can onto the porch and the front walls of the guest house.

Jupe smelled gasoline.

Letitia Radford hurled the can through the open door onto the ants that swarmed and pulsed in the living room of the little house. Then she took something out of her sweater pocket.

"Letitia! No!" Woolley leaped forward.

She struck a match and tossed it.

There was a sound like a giant puff. The front porch of the cottage was suddenly in flames. They spread, leaping, to the living room.

"There!" she cried. "That will fix them. I've had enough. I can't stand any more!"

And she turned and marched up the hill.

16

A Scare in the Night

"If only I'd gotten the license number of that truck," moaned Pete. "It was dumb not to get the license number!"

It was the morning after the fire at the Radford estate. The Three Investigators were in their office in Headquarters, talking over the events of the day before.

"A pool maintenance man," said Bob. "Now that we know what he does, it might not be that hard to locate him."

"We may not need to," said Jupe. "Pete, you said you were knocked out for only a few seconds, and when you came to, the man was running down the road after his truck."

Pete nodded. "He caught it when it ran into the ditch and stopped. Then he climbed in and drove away quick, brakes or no brakes."

"Then the mysterious pool man is not the scarecrow," said Jupiter. "Because at the moment he was chasing his truck down the road, the scarecrow was trying to break into Dr. Woolley's laboratory."

"Then who *is* the scarecrow?" asked Pete.

"The Burroughs couple are in the clear," Jupe summarized. "I saw them in the Radford house just moments before I saw the scarecrow. Dr. Woolley is unaccounted for at that time, but he was with us when we saw the scarecrow the other night. That leaves Gerhart Malz, who seems a most unlikely suspect."

Jupe leaned forward and put his elbows on the desk. "We could discuss this case forever and never reach a conclusion," he said. "We simply don't know enough. I suggest we try another approach. Letitia Radford is the victim of the attacks. By now she must have recovered from her hysteria of last evening. I think we should question her about people who might have a reason to upset her."

"She'll get hysterical all over again," warned Pete.

Bob nodded. "She thinks she's a nice, lovable lady. Can she face the fact that other people might dislike her?"

"Well, she can't help knowing that at least one person is against her—the scarecrow!" Jupe pointed out. "I think we should talk to her. Let's go now, while Aunt Mathilda is marketing."

"Good thinking," said Pete. "Aunt Mathilda will put us to work if she sees us!"

In a few minutes the boys were pedaling up the Coast Highway on their bikes. Letitia Radford answered the door when they rang the bell at the Radford house. As usual, she was carefully dressed. But she looked very pale, and there were dark shadows under her eyes.

"We wondered if we could talk with you, Miss Radford," said Jupiter.

"Well, I suppose. If you must. I'm awfully tired. The fire chief was here until late last night. He was quite angry with me." She grimaced. "He thinks there are better ways to get rid of ants than setting a house on fire."

Jupe nodded but didn't say anything. He agreed with the fire chief.

"I didn't get much sleep anyway. Mrs. Chumley wasn't feeling well last night. She's in pain some of the time, and she doesn't like to be alone then. I was sitting up with her. In fact, I was with her just now when the doorbell rang."

"Would you like me to sit with her for a while?" Bob offered. "You could probably use a break."

Letitia smiled wanly. "That would be nice. She's in her sitting room. Just knock before you go in."

Bob went toward the back of the house, to Mrs. Chumley's suite, and Letitia led the other two boys into the living room. She sat down on a sofa and motioned the boys to take chairs.

"We wanted to talk to you about people you have known," Jupe said. "Can you think of anyone who might have a grudge against you?"

"A grudge against *me*?"

Jupe nodded. "What about Gerhart Malz?"

"Don't be ridiculous! Gerry's practically a member of the household. Besides, he only cares about his paintings."

"Perhaps someone who works here has a grudge."

"You can't mean Burroughs!" said Letitia.

"Oh no! We're quite sure that Burroughs is not the scarecrow. But couldn't there be someone else? How about the gardeners? I understand they come twice a week. And what about the pool man? Doesn't he come regularly, too?"

"Twice a week," said Letitia. "But why should he dislike me? I don't really know him. He's a student at U.C.L.A., I understand. One of those sun-bronzed boys who run around without a shirt."

"A young man?" Jupe looked startled.

"Of course. I said he was a student, didn't I?"

Jupe frowned and began to pull at his lower lip.

"It isn't any use," said Letitia. "And it doesn't matter, really, because I'm not going to be here much longer. I'm going back to Europe. The scarecrow . . . well, he came back last night."

Jupiter and Pete looked at her questioningly.

"About midnight," she said. "I was in Mrs. Chumley's room and the lights were out. I saw him out on the driveway. He was pushing a wheelbarrow down toward the garage."

"A wheelbarrow?" echoed Jupe. "An empty wheelbarrow? Or was there something in it?"

"There was a pile of something," said Letitia. "It

was too dark to see exactly what. Dirt, maybe."

"Didn't you call anyone?" asked Jupiter.

"No. I'm sick of calling people." Her tone was bleak. "If I'm going crazy, I'll do it quietly from now on. The other way doesn't get me anywhere."

"I see," said Jupe.

"And I don't know anyone who would have a grudge against me. It would have to be a very old grudge. I haven't spent much time in Los Angeles for years."

Mrs. Burroughs came to the doorway between the living room and the dining room. "Excuse me, miss," she said. "Burroughs is going into Rocky Beach to the market. Is there anything you want?"

"Some more aspirin, Mrs. Burroughs, if you please," said Letitia.

"Certainly, miss."

Mrs. Burroughs went away, and Letitia stood up. "Are you boys going to stay for a while?" she asked. "I'd like it if you would. I feel safer somehow with you here."

"Of course," said Jupe. "Where is Dr. Woolley, by the way?"

"After I burned down the guest house, he moved into the barn," said Letitia. "I imagine he's there now, getting some rest. And I think I'll get some rest, too."

She started for the hall, then hesitated. "I think I'll ask Mrs. Burroughs to go upstairs with me," she said. "I don't feel safe alone."

"Good idea," said Jupe.

Letitia went to the kitchen. A moment later Pete and Jupe heard Mrs. Burroughs exclaiming in her usual hearty way. She and Letitia went up the stairs. Jupe strolled to a front window and saw a big black Buick drive away down Chaparral Canyon.

"Burroughs just left for town," said Jupe, "and the car he's driving is riding low."

Bob came in from the hall just then. "Mrs. Chumley's asleep now," he said. "She took a pill for the pain."

He paused. "Funny," he said. "Just before she had me wheel her into her bedroom and help her to bed, she told me about the real Vermeer that hangs upstairs in the museum. She also mentioned the candelabra outside, and described how its prisms vibrate every time the grandfather clock on the landing strikes the hour."

Pete stared. "She said that? But—but she can't climb stairs! How could she know?"

"No doubt Gerhart Malz told her," said Jupe indifferently. "He seems completely intrigued with that candelabra." Jupe paused, and his eyes lit up. "Now, Mrs. Chumley is sleeping. Letitia and Mrs. Burroughs are upstairs and Burroughs is in town. The coast is clear, fellows! We can do what we should have done a long time ago."

"What's that?" asked Pete.

"Search the house!" said Jupiter.

17

Caught!

The Three Investigators moved quietly through the big house. They were mindful of Letitia Radford and Mrs. Burroughs upstairs, and of Mrs. Chumley in her suite on the first floor. Stealthily they opened cupboards and closets, peered into drawers, and felt along the tops of cabinets.

They found nothing in the kitchen or the pantry that could be a clue to the identity of the scarecrow. The small servants' sitting room beyond the kitchen was also innocent. So were the two bedrooms in the servants' wing. There were uniforms in the closet of one of the rooms, and a few dresses and a sports jacket and some slacks, but there was no burlap sack and no black hat which might have made up a scarecrow.

"But we know that Burroughs isn't the scarecrow!" protested Bob. "Why are we doing this?"

"It would be foolish not to," said Jupiter. "We've been so afraid of upsetting Letitia Radford that we

112

haven't been at all thorough. Never mind. I didn't think we'd find anything significant here. Now we go to the basement."

The cellar of the big house was divided into a number of rooms. The boys found a wine cellar, a furnace room, several storage rooms, and a workshop. Then Jupe led the others to the corner of the house directly beneath Mrs. Chumley's bedroom, where the door he'd seen the night before opened onto the lawn. At this spot the ground outside was almost exactly level with the basement floor.

"See that?" Jupe spoke very softly as he pointed to tire tracks on the cement floor. "The scarecrow pushed his wheelbarrow out this way—a wheelbarrow with a rubber tire. It was loaded with dirt. See the bits of mud on the floor?"

"But where did the dirt come from?" Bob wondered.

The boys left the outer door and began to follow the tire tracks back through the basement. The telltale bits of clay on the floor led them to a narrow corridor that ran between an unused storeroom and a room with a heavy, thick door. Pete switched on the light in the latter room, and the boys saw dusty pipes on the ceiling of the chamber.

"It must have been a meat locker once," said Pete. "It's like the cold room at the Rocky Beach Market, only not as big."

"This house must have been something in the days when the Radford family really lived here," said Bob. "Imagine! Your own private cold-storage room!"

Jupe nodded, but he wasn't paying attention to Bob. He was looking quite satisfied, as if he had just found exactly what he'd hoped to find. He gestured toward the end of the corridor. "Look! That's where the dirt came from!"

Pete and Bob stared. There should have been cement blocks at the end of this corridor—the cement blocks that made up the outer wall of the basement. Instead there was a gaping black hole.

"A tunnel!" said Pete.

Jupe took a flashlight out of his pocket. "I found this in a drawer in the kitchen," he told his companions. "I thought we might need it."

He snapped the light on and pointed its beam into the tunnel.

"Wow!" said Bob. "Someone really worked on that! Look at the timbers bracing the ceiling!"

"Like a mine tunnel," said Pete. "So *that's* what the scarecrow's been doing. But . . . but . . ."

He stopped, bewildered.

"But it doesn't make sense for the scarecrow to invade someone's house to build a tunnel, does it?" said Jupiter. "He would certainly be discovered."

"So someone in the house is the scarecrow," Pete decided. "Or someone in the house is in cahoots with the scarecrow. Burroughs and his wife!"

"That seems like a logical conclusion," said Jupe. "And we can guess where this tunnel leads!"

Bob studied the wall. It was on the side of the house facing the road. "The tunnel goes under the road to the Mosby place," he said. His voice was almost a whisper. "Someone's going to break into the Mosby Museum!"

"Shall we check it out?" suggested Jupiter.

He went into the tunnel, crouching, shining his light to left and to right.

The other two boys followed him. No one spoke, and the dirt floor absorbed the sound of the steps. The air became rather stale as they went on. After what seemed like hours of shuffling through the dark passageway, Jupe stopped. His way was blocked by a cement wall. He touched it. It was solid—still whole. "The basement of the Mosby house," he whispered. "This is the only portion of the museum that isn't guarded. There are burglar alarms everywhere else."

Bob and Pete nodded. Jupe handed the light back to Bob, who turned and began to lead the way out of the tunnel to the Radford house.

"That's unreal!" exclaimed Pete, when the three boys were once again in the Radford basement. "It must have taken months to dig that tunnel!"

"Now we know why the scarecrow was trying to frighten Letitia away," said Jupe. "He was afraid she might come to the basement and discover the tunnel—or that she might look out one night and see something."

Bob snapped off the flashlight, and the boys started back through the corridor toward the stairs. "Now I understand why the car Burroughs drove into

Rocky Beach was riding so low," said Jupe. "He's been loading the dirt from the tunnel into the trunk of the car and taking it away."

The boys came abreast of the abandoned cold-storage room. Pete stopped and sniffed.

"Something's burning!" he said.

He reached around the edge of the doorway and flipped the light switch.

The old refrigerator room was misty with smoke. There were heaps of rags in a corner, and a couple of old paint cans with the lids off.

"Good night!" said Pete. "Somebody left a bunch of paint rags here. Internal combustion's started!"

He crossed the refrigerator room and kicked at the rags. They flew this way and that, and flames leaped up from several of them.

"Watch it!" said Bob. He jumped to stamp out the little fires, and Jupe hurried to help.

Suddenly, from the corridor there came a low, eerie laugh.

The three boys spun around.

The scarecrow stood staring at them. Its painted grin was ghastly in the light from the naked bulb in the ceiling. For a moment it did not move. Then it pulled at the heavy door and slammed it shut.

"No! Wait!" Pete jumped to the door, seized the handle, and pulled.

The door didn't budge.

"Stop!" cried Pete again. "Come back!"

"Save your breath," said Jupe. "He isn't going to let us out of here. Not now. Maybe not ever!"

18

The Break-In

Bob examined the latch on the inside of the door. "Just our luck!" he said. "It's broken!"

"I don't believe it's a matter of luck at all," said Jupiter. "I think that the scarecrow saw us go into the tunnel. He decided that we knew too much, and he broke the latch. He then decoyed us in here by setting those rags on fire."

"It was dumb to fall for that," said Pete, "but I didn't want to see the house burn down."

"The scarecrow was counting on that," said Jupe. "And he's counting on this room to keep us quiet. I mean, it won't do us any good to yell or pound and try to attract someone's attention. This room is too well insulated. No one would hear."

"Not even if we bang on the pipes on the ceiling?" asked Pete. "Wouldn't they carry sound out of the room?"

Jupe nodded. "But those pipes aren't connected to the rest of the house. They just run to a refrigeration unit, which is sure to be somewhere right outside. No one would hear us banging unless he was already close by in the basement."

Pete sat down on the floor. "Is the scarecrow just going to leave us here?"

"Someone will come looking for us," said Jupiter confidently. "We left our bicycles out in front, right near Letitia's car. She's bound to see them."

"Would she come down here?" wondered Bob. "To the basement? With the spiders?"

Jupe thought about it. "No, she wouldn't," he said glumly. "Anyway, if she sees the bikes she'll just think we're with Dr. Woolley. And if Burroughs or his wife notices the bikes—well, we certainly can't count on them for help."

The boys sat still after that. The silence in the room was so intense that it seemed to close in on them, muffling their thoughts.

"Aunt Mathilda will guess where we are," Jupe said at last. "She'll send Hans or Konrad. Or she'll call Chief Reynolds, and *he'll* guess we're in the Radford house. But that could take hours. . . ."

Jupe didn't bother to go on. The Investigators were all wondering the same thing—whether the air in the room would last until they were found.

Time crept by, one slow hour after another. Jupe's stomach began rumbling. He wondered if dinnertime was close. Or was he hungry because he'd missed lunch?

Suddenly the boys felt a tremor in the room.

"What was that?" asked Pete in alarm, sitting up straight.

"Probably a little earthquake," answered Bob.

"Oh, great!" muttered Pete as he slumped back against the wall. "It's not enough to be trapped in an airless room! Now we can get buried alive in an earthquake, too!"

The minutes dragged by. Hours seemed to pass.

"Am I imagining it," asked Bob finally, "or is the air in here beginning to get stale?"

"It can't be!" said Jupiter. "We haven't been here—" He stopped and held his breath for an instant. "What was that?" he whispered.

The other two boys listened.

"Someone's banging on something," Pete decided. He got up and went to the door.

"Hey!" he yelled. "Hey, we're in here!" He pounded on the door with his fist.

Jupe took off a shoe, stood up, and began to bang it on the door. All three boys yelled at once.

And at last the big door to the cold room swung open. The boys saw a tall man with bushy white hair standing in the doorway. His skin was leathery from long exposure to the sun, and deep furrows ran from his nose down to the corners of his mouth. Letitia Radford clung to his arm.

"Thank heavens!" he said. "I knew you had to be here someplace. I saw you arrive, but you never left!"

Jupiter grinned and walked out into the corridor.

"Obviously there are advantages to having a mystery man who keeps watch over this house."

"Mystery man?" said Letitia Radford. "He's not a mystery man. He's Ben Agnier. He used to be our pool man. I wish somebody would tell me what's going on here. Where are Burroughs and Mrs. Burroughs? I woke up from my nap and everyone was gone!"

"If Burroughs and his wife are gone, then their business here is finished," said Jupiter. He nodded toward the tunnel at the end of the corridor.

Agnier followed his glance. "So that's what they were up to!" he said. "A tunnel!"

"To the Mosby house," Jupe told him.

Jupe snapped on his flashlight and started through the tunnel. The others followed.

"Wait!" cried Letitia Radford. "Don t leave me!"

"Then hurry along!" said Agnier.

Letitia scurried after Bob, who had been the last to enter the tunnel.

There seemed to be no reason for stealth, yet no one spoke until they reached the end of the tunnel. There they saw a large opening in the concrete wall that separated the underground passage from the Mosby basement. An acrid odor lingered in the air.

"Dynamite, I imagine," said Agnier. His long, brown face was grim.

"Of course!" exclaimed Jupiter. "We felt the explosion earlier. It must have taken place after five, when the guards go home."

Agnier went through the opening into the Mosby

basement and, in the light from Jupe's flashlight, found a light switch. In the cellar were packing crates and a furnace room and a room with the elaborate machinery that kept the temperature in the house at a constant level. Agnier and the boys glanced around quickly and then went upstairs, with a silent, pale Letitia Radford staying close to them.

"Mr. Malz!" shouted Jupiter when they reached the entrance hall.

No one answered.

"Maybe he wasn't here when they broke in," said Pete.

They moved on through the rooms on the lower floor. Nothing was disturbed there. Again and again they called for Malz. The house was perfectly silent.

Was Gerhart Malz still in the museum? Was he hidden away, as the boys had been, and left to suffocate or starve? Jupe shuddered. The tunnel-makers were without pity.

"Mr. Malz!" Jupe shouted, and started up the stairs.

The rooms on the second floor were stripped almost bare. The Vermeer was gone. So were the Rembrandts from the next room, and the Van Dyke and the Reubens. So were the ancient Flemish paintings that had glowed with rich, intricate color. Room after room was empty and echoing.

"A fortune!" said Jupe. "They took a fortune in art!"

Letitia Radford gazed at the blank white walls.

"The entire Mosby collection of paintings," she said. "Burroughs and Mrs. Burroughs? The house-man and the cook? They dug that tunnel and . . . and Burroughs was the scarecrow after all?"

There was a thumping from overhead.

"Aha!" said Jupe.

He darted up the stairs to the third floor, where Gerhart Malz had his workshop and his private rooms. The thumping grew louder as he went. Jupe followed the sound, with Bob and Pete close behind him, and opened the door to a closet in the small bedroom to the left of the stairs.

Gerhart Malz was there, bound with clothesline and gagged with a towel.

"It's okay, Mr. Malz," said Jupe. He knelt beside the curator. "We'll have you loose in a second!"

19

The Watcher's Story

"I would appreciate it greatly if someone would tell me exactly what is going on here!"

Mrs. Chumley sat upright in her wheelchair, her hands nervously clutching the afghan that covered her knees. Her eyes were sharp with curiosity.

"I was worried about you, Mrs. Chumley," said Ben Agnier. The tall man sat in an armchair in Mrs. Chumley's room. Gerhart Malz was there, too. So was Letitia Radford, and so were The Three Investigators. They could hear police moving about in the cellar below, taking pictures, gathering evidence. More officers were busy across the road in the Mosby house.

"What has become of Burroughs?" Mrs. Chumley demanded. "And Mrs. Burroughs? Letitia, it's time for dinner! And we never had our tea!"

"I'll put a kettle on," said Letitia. But she didn't move. She had taken a small armchair near Ben

Agnier, and she was staring at him with a mixture of curiosity and admiration.

"You were watching this house?" she said. "How terribly clever of you."

Agnier's face flushed. "Not—not really," he said. "I was just worried about Mrs. Chumley."

"That was extremely thoughtful of you, Ben," said Mrs. Chumley. "But why were you worried about me?"

"Well, I didn't like that Burroughs," said Ben Agnier. "Everything changed after he came."

"Things *did* change," admitted Mrs. Chumley. "I thought they got better. It was a joy to have competent servants in the house again. You can't imagine, Letitia. I've had six or seven couples since your mother died, and none of them at all satisfactory—until Burroughs and his wife."

"Your precious couple were nothing but thieves!" said Mr. Malz, and he told her about the tunnel.

"You mean to tell me that they were digging a tunnel the whole time they were here!" exclaimed Mrs. Chumley. "I don't know when they could have done it. Really, I don't!"

"Probably at night, Mrs. Chumley, when you were asleep," said Jupiter.

"The very idea makes me tired," said Mrs. Chumley. "When did they sleep, for goodness' sake?"

"They didn't always dig at night," Agnier told her. "Sometimes they worked in the daytime. That's how I got fired."

"I don't understand," said Mrs. Chumley. "Burroughs told me that you were giving up your pool service—retiring—so we got that new young man."

"Burroughs fired me," Agnier declared. "I saw him coming out of the basement one morning wearing work clothes. He was wheeling a barrow loaded with dirt. Now, you don't see a butler or a houseman pushing a wheelbarrow every day of the week. I asked him what was up, and he said that the cellar wall had given way in one place and dumped a pile of dirt on the floor.

"I didn't believe him. I've been in the basement of this house, and the walls aren't about to give way. When I told him that, he fired me!

"Well, I figured if I was going to be fired, you could fire me, Mrs. Chumley, not Burroughs. So I went around and rang the front doorbell. Only Mrs. Burroughs answered and she said you were sleeping and couldn't be disturbed. Every time I tried to see you after that, Mrs. Burroughs got in the way. If I called, Burroughs answered the telephone. I wrote a couple of notes, but I don't suppose you ever received them."

Mrs. Chumley shook her head. "Good heavens!" she exclaimed. "I've practically been a prisoner of those two thieves! They might have killed me!"

"I didn't think they'd do that," said Ben Agnier, "but I was worried. I started watching this place from the old house on Rock Rim Drive. I'd stop there every day and stay until I saw you on the terrace. As long as you looked okay, I figured everything was really all right.

"Then that baldheaded guy came and planted that cornfield, and about that time old Jason Creel, who'd been head gardener here for more than twenty years—well, he got fired."

"I fired Jason myself," said Mrs. Chumley. "The poor man had gotten careless. And he didn't need the work."

"I know that," said Agnier. "He'd only been coming here out of loyalty. But he didn't like Burroughs, either.

"And then Miss Letitia came home, and every day I could see her out on the terrace. And it came to me that you and Miss Letitia were awfully isolated. Nobody from outside ever came, except you, Mr. Malz, and the guy who planted all that corn."

"Someone mention me?" said Charles Woolley. The entomologist was standing in the doorway. "The police have been to see me," he said. "I told them where I've been all day, and they said I could come up here and wait with you. I think they want me out of the way."

He bowed to Ben Agnier. "Please don't let me interrupt you."

"I was about finished," said Agnier.

"But if you were so worried," said Letitia Radford, "why didn't you come up and talk to us when you saw us on the terrace?"

"I felt foolish," said Agnier. "I did try to come one day and I almost bumped into the boys." He nodded at the Investigators. "Gave me a scare when you chased me."

"But what about the scarecrow?" said Letitia. "What did you think when you saw the scarecrow?"

"Only scarecrow I ever saw was that one on the fence," Agnier declared.

"But I'll tell you one thing," he went on. "I was kind of glad when you boys took to hanging around. You gave the women some contact with the outside world. But when you came here earlier today and you didn't leave again, I got uneasy. When Burroughs took your bikes and wheeled them to the garage, I realized I hadn't seen Miss Letitia on the terrace, and I hadn't seen Mrs. Chumley. I kept watching, and Burroughs went off and came back with a rental trailer.

"I couldn't figure out what a houseman wanted with a trailer. I kept watching. A couple of hours after Burroughs brought that trailer, he and Mrs. Burroughs left with it—bag and baggage and a lot besides. I couldn't see exactly what they'd loaded in that thing, but it was full!"

"With a few million dollars in beautiful paintings!" said Gerhart Malz.

"Whatever it was, it looked queer to me," said Agnier. "I came up the hill to the house. The doors were locked, but I broke one of the windows on the terrace and got in that way."

"And you woke me," said Letitia, "and we woke Mrs. Chumley, but at first we couldn't find the boys. Ben thought of the cellar, and there they were in the old refrigerator room."

"Thank goodness you looked," said Jupe. He got up and went to the fireplace, glancing at the wall above the mantel. There was a strip of unfaded wallpaper around the frame of the Vermeer copy. "We probably forced Mr. and Mrs. Burroughs to act today," he said. "Once we got to the basement and saw the tunnel, they had to put us out of the way and move fast."

There was a quick rap on the door, and Chief Reynolds came in. "My men will be through downstairs very soon," he said. "The reporters will probably be here any minute. I can make a statement if you don't want to see them."

"Please do," said Mrs. Chumley. "And Letitia, you were going to put the kettle on. I would so love a cup of tea."

"I'll do it, Mrs. Chumley," said Jupiter.

He went to the door and paused, then went out. Pete and Bob exchanged glances. Jupe had been pulling at his lower lip as he went, and they knew what that meant. He was concentrating on some problem. Some new idea had occurred to him.

Pete shrugged after a moment, and Bob sighed. Jupiter would never tell them his ideas until he was good and ready!

20

Jupe Makes Deductions

Jupe sat down at the kitchen table to wait for the kettle to boil. A telephone was on the table, trailing a cord from the jack near the pantry door. By the phone lay a newspaper, folded back to the crossword puzzle. When Jupe lifted the newspaper he saw a scratch pad underneath it.

Someone had doodled on the pad. There were hearts pierced with arrows. There were dollar signs. Several times over, there was the word "Vermeer."

And there was a telephone number.

"Aha!" said Jupe. He picked up the telephone and dialed the number. There were two rings at the other end, and then a click. "Short-Haul Trailer Company," said a voice. "Can I help you?"

"You already have," said Jupiter. He put down the telephone and scowled at a notation in a corner of the pad.

"Golden Fleece," someone had written. "Pana-manian reg."

The teakettle on the stove began to whistle. Jupiter ignored it. He was grinning happily and leafing through the newspaper.

"Hey, what's the matter?" Bob appeared in the doorway. "The water's boiling! Are you deaf?"

Jupe didn't answer, and Bob went to the stove and turned off the heat under the kettle.

"Jupe?" Pete had come into the kitchen. "What is it? What's up?"

"I've got it!" shouted Jupe. "Chief Reynolds!"

He jumped up and began to run—and almost collided with the chief in the kitchen doorway.

"Well?" said Chief Reynolds.

"Look!" Jupe was so excited that his hands shook. "The note pad. Golden Fleece! You see that there? And here in the paper in the shipping news. The *Golden Fleece*, sailing under Panamanian registry, is due to leave San Pedro at nine-fifteen this evening. Chief, that's less than an hour from now!"

Chief Reynolds seized the note pad. "Where'd you find this?" he demanded.

"Right here next to the telephone. The number on the pad is the number of the Short-Haul Trailer Company.

"Chief Reynolds, whoever rented the trailer sat here at the telephone and called. He—or she—also noted that the *Golden Fleece* sails under Panamani-an registry. Lots of ships do. The Burroughs couple were making last-minute plans to get the paintings out of the country. They're headed wherever the *Golden Fleece* is going!"

"I'll be switched!" said Chief Reynolds.

"You have to stop that ship!" cried Jupiter.

Chief Reynolds picked up the telephone and dialed the operator. He demanded to be connected immediately with the harbor master at San Pedro. When he got the harbor master, he identified himself and demanded that the *Golden Fleece* be delayed.

"I'll be there in half an hour," he said, "but you'd better not let that ship cast off!"

He then hung up the telephone.

Gerhart Malz came into the kitchen. "Mrs. Chumley sent me to find out what's going on here," he said. "I've never seen a woman so eager for her tea."

"Jupiter will make the tea in a minute," said Chief Reynolds. "I want you, Malz."

"What?" Malz looked startled.

"I want you to come with me to San Pedro. Jupiter here thinks that our criminals are aboard a ship called the *Golden Fleece*. I've asked that she not be allowed to sail before I get there. You can come with me to identify the stolen paintings—if they're aboard."

"My word!" said Malz.

"Don't we get to go?" cried Pete. "Or Jupe at least? He found the clue, didn't he?"

"And he will be the first one I call when we have the paintings," said Chief Reynolds. "Come along, Mr. Malz." He took the curator by the arm and ushered him out the kitchen door.

"Well, darn!" cried Pete. "That's not fair!"

Jupiter said nothing. He put the kettle on again, and when it boiled he made tea. Bob found cups and saucers and some little cakes, and Pete discovered a plate of sandwiches in the refrigerator. The boys put everything on a tray and Pete carried it to Mrs. Chumley's room.

"How nice," said Mrs. Chumley. "I'm simply starving. Letitia, we've had almost nothing to eat today."

"I'm not hungry," said Letitia Radford.

"I am," Mrs. Chumley declared. "My, these little cakes look good. Will you have some, Mr. Woolley? And Ben, how about you? Boys? And where is Gerry Malz? Doesn't he want his tea?"

"He and Chief Reynolds have left for San Pedro," said Jupe. "They're going to see if Burroughs and his wife are on board a ship called the *Golden Fleece*."

Mrs. Chumley had started to pour a cup of tea. She stopped and put the teapot down on the tray, as if the task were suddenly too much for her.

"While the chief is gone, perhaps we can have a talk, Mrs. Chumley," said Jupe, "and you can tell us how you and the Burroughs couple agreed on your share of the loot!"

21

An Unexpected Exit

Letitia Radford had been lounging on the sofa opposite Mrs. Chumley. She sat up straight now. "I don't think I heard right," she said. "Would you mind repeating that?"

"I said that I want to discuss how Mrs. Chumley and the Burroughs couple agreed on her share of the loot from the robbery." Jupe's round face was solemn.

Pete and Bob took seats near the window. The summer twilight was deepening, blurring objects in the room, but no one moved to turn on a light.

"You were the one who made the robbery possible," said Jupe to Mrs. Chumley. "It couldn't have happened without your knowledge."

"Young man, you are impertinent," said Mrs. Chumley. "When Chief Reynolds returns, I'm going to speak to him. He'll see to it that you never set foot on this property again."

"Possibly he will," said Jupiter, "but there's another possibility, and that is that Burroughs and his wife will confess and you will be implicated."

"That's ridiculous!" Letitia Radford stood up and went to Mrs. Chumley. "Why should Mrs. Chumley steal? She has everything! She just has to wish for a thing and my brother will get it for her. We're her family! This is her home!"

"Watch yourself, Jupiter," warned Charles Woolley. The entomologist had been sitting quietly in a far corner of the room. He reached out now and turned on the lamp on the table nearest him. "You'd better have a good reason for your accusation!"

"I think I do," said Jupe. "Several reasons."

He turned to the woman in the wheelchair. "How could you live for more than six months with a couple who were digging a tunnel and not know about it? Couldn't you hear them or see them at work? The dirt from the tunnel went out through a door that is directly under your bedroom."

"I sleep quite soundly," said Mrs. Chumley.

"Not always. Last night you kept Miss Radford with you because you couldn't sleep. Or you claimed you couldn't sleep. Perhaps you only wanted to keep Miss Radford busy.

"Then this morning you told Bob about the candelabra that is just outside the Vermeer room in the Mosby Museum. You described the way the prisms on the candelabra vibrate when the grandfather clock strikes. Mr. Malz said that candelabra is a new acquisition. If you never climb stairs, as you say, how did you know about it?"

Mrs. Chumley looked startled. "Well, I . . . I suppose Gerry told me about it."

"I would accept that if it weren't for the snapshots," said Jupiter.

"Snapshots?" repeated Mrs. Chumley.

"Last night we were patrolling the grounds, trying to catch a glimpse of the scarecrow, and you had left your drapes open. You were playing chess with Mr. Malz. After he left, you went into your bedroom, didn't you?"

"Perhaps I did. What about it?"

"You opened your closet. From where I stood I could see boxes piled on the shelf in your closet."

"Well?" said Mrs. Chumley.

"Then you closed your drapes, so I didn't see what you did next. However, a few moments later you came into the living room with a large box filled with snapshots.

"I didn't have time to think about those snapshots last night, because I saw the scarecrow almost immediately after you brought them to Miss Radford. Today, however, while we were locked in the cold room downstairs, I had ample time to think about them. Mrs. Chumley, how did you get that box down off the closet shelf?"

Mrs. Chumley frowned as if she were trying to remember. "I suppose I used my yardstick," she said at last. "I keep a yardstick in the corner of the closet. When I want to get something down I pry it off the shelf with the yardstick and catch it as it falls. It saves calling someone every time I need something."

"No," said Jupe. "You didn't do that with a box of snapshots. Snapshots are heavy. They'd have hurt you if they dropped on you, and they'd have spilled. No, Mrs. Chumley, you stood up and lifted those snapshots down."

"Ridiculous!" said Mrs. Chumley. "I cannot stand. Everyone knows that. Not since my accident."

"You knew how terrified Miss Radford is of scarecrows," Jupe went on. "You also knew of her fear of insects. Mrs. Chumley, it was you who invented the scarecrow."

"No!" cried Letitia Radford. "That's impossible!"

"It is not impossible," said Jupe. "It's quite logical. What's more, on at least one occasion you were the scarecrow. It was you who locked us in the cold room, Mrs. Chumley!"

"You're an impudent young pup!" snapped Mrs. Chumley, "and I'm not going to listen to another word you say. I am going to bed." -

"Wait!" said Jupe. "I haven't—"

"That's enough, Jupiter," said Dr. Woolley sternly. "All you've told us are guesses and bits of circumstantial evidence. You haven't got a solid reason for accusing Mrs. Chumley of anything!"

"Yes, I have," said Jupe. "I saved the best reason

for last. Would you like to hear it, Mrs. Chumley?"

"I would like you to go to the devil!" cried Mrs. Chumley. She swung her wheelchair around and started for the bedroom door.

"Wait," said Letitia Radford. "I'll help you."

Mrs. Chumley looked back at the younger woman. There was concern on Letitia Radford's face, but there was also doubt.

"Never mind," said Mrs. Chumley. "I can manage by myself."

"You know you can't" said Letitia, but Mrs. Chumley was gone. The bedroom door closed behind her.

"Could she have done those terrible things?" said Letitia. "She couldn't have! It's not possible—"

Letitia broke off. A terrible scream came from Mrs. Chumley's room.

Pete jumped up, and Jupe started toward the bedroom door. But before either of the boys could reach it, the door was flung open.

"You young beast!" shrieked Mrs. Chumley. She was standing up, her face blazing with rage and her chest heaving. She held a pillow in one hand. "You did that on purpose!"

She swung the pillow. It caught Jupiter on the side of the head. He staggered aside, and before anyone else could move, Mrs. Chumley ran. The sitting room door banged behind her. Then the front door of the house opened and crashed shut again.

"She can walk!" cried Ben Agnier. "She's not a cripple at all!"

The group in the sitting room heard a car start in front of the house.

"Oh, dear!" said Letitia Radford. "I left the keys in my car. Mrs. Chumley always scolded me about that. She said . . . she said that someday someone would steal the car."

Charles Woolley snorted.

Pete had gone a step or two into the bedroom. Now he made a horrified sound and backed out.

"Dr. Woolley," he said. "Look!"

Charles Woolley hurried to the doorway, and the others crowded to peer over his shoulder.

Streaming across the floor were thousands upon thousands of ants. They came from an open window, and were marching up over the bed.

"Another colony!" said Woolley, his voice filled with delight. "No wonder she ran. I might have run myself!"

22

A Final Surprise

It was nearly midnight when Chief Reynolds and Gerhart Malz returned to the Radford house with the news that Burroughs and his wife were in custody.

"Were all the paintings recovered?" asked Jupe.

"Yes, we got them," said Malz. "They're under guard in San Pedro tonight. Tomorrow they'll be returned to the museum."

The curator yawned. He looked very weary. "Where's Mrs. Chumley?" he asked. "Did she go to bed?"

Letitia Radford and Charles Woolley told him what had happened. They told about Jupiter's accusation and the ants in the bedroom, which Woolley had repulsed with insect spray, and about Mrs. Chumley's flight in Letitia's car.

"There's a bulletin out on the car," Jupiter told Chief Reynolds. "Mrs. Chumley won't get far."

"You mean she isn't crippled?" said Malz.

"She ran like a rabbit," Pete told him.

"But why did she put on an act like that?" said Malz. "She's been in that wheelchair for years!"

He turned to Letitia. "Did she need money?"

"Hardly," said Letitia. "My mother was very generous. She remembered everyone in her will—especially Mrs. Chumley. Yet Mrs. Chumley was the scarecrow. Isn't that dreadful? We found the costume in her closet." Letitia did not look tearful now. She looked angry. "It was cruel!" she said. "She did that to me after I treated her like a mother! I really did!"

"She may have felt trapped," said Jupiter. "We won't know the full story until she is caught and confesses, but we can guess what happened."

Jupiter leaned back in his chair and began to speak slowly, working out the details as he went along.

"Mrs. Chumley must have felt threatened when Mrs. Radford died," he said. "There was no longer any real need to keep this house open, but this house was Mrs. Chumley's home. No doubt Mrs. Chumley feared that she would have to leave here and go to live in some little apartment in Los Angeles. She would be lonely, since she seems to have few friends of her own. And her life wouldn't be nearly as comfortable.

"Then she had an accident and she broke her hips. It must have started her thinking. We all know about people who have minor automobile accidents and then claim that the whiplash has injured them and their necks hurt. Who can prove that their necks don't hurt? If Mrs. Chumley insisted that her legs wouldn't support her, who could say she was wrong?"

"So she lied to my brother and he kept the house open just for her!" Letitia Radford said bitterly. "And with the Radfords away, she became the head of the house, didn't she? With servants waiting on her hand and foot! She must have hated it every time I came home!"

"I doubt that she minded until Burroughs and his wife began work on that tunnel," said Jupe. "It must have been very difficult for them to dig while you were here, so they tried to frighten you away with the scarecrow and the bugs.

"It was a marvelous coincidence that they were all about the same build. They could all wear the scarecrow costume. That way they could alibi one another.

"The night we saw the scarecrow with the scythe, Mrs. Chumley and Burroughs were already with you at the front of the house. The scarecrow that night had to be Mrs. Burroughs. She ran from us in the darkness and doubled back to the rear of the house. She went through the cellar door, shucked the scarecrow outfit, made a quick call to the police in Rocky Beach, then hurried into the living room with her cap all askew. She claimed to have seen the scarecrow out the window, so we assumed she'd been in the house all along."

"But what about the night the scarecrow tried to break into Charles Woolley's lab again?" asked Bob. "When you saw the scarecrow that night, Mrs. Burroughs was in the kitchen and Burroughs was watching TV in the servants' quarters, and Mrs. Chumley was in the living room with Miss Radford."

"Suppose it wasn't Burroughs watching television," said Jupe. "Suppose he'd rigged up a dummy that would look like a man watching television. He knew that anyone in the living room could look out across the pool to the servants' quarters. He'd rig a dummy if he wanted an alibi while he was stealing some more insects from Charles Woolley.

"And today the scarecrow who locked us in the cold room was Mrs. Chumley. Her room is on the first floor. She could have heard us in the cellar. Or perhaps it was Mrs. Burroughs. It doesn't matter. They were all in it together."

"But she didn't need anything," said Letitia Radford. "Why would she hire a couple of thieves to help rob a museum?"

"I think Burroughs and his wife thought of the robbery first," said Jupe. "I think they took the job here because the Mosby Museum was so near. They must have been delighted that the only resident of the house was a crippled woman who could not come downstairs to the cellar.

"At some point they must have discovered that Mrs. Chumley could walk, and she must have discovered that they were digging. They came to terms. She would pretend ignorance of their activities. In return, they would not reveal the fact that she had been duping the Radford family for years. When you came home, Miss Radford, they had already joined forces. They felt you were a threat, and the showing of *The Wizard of Oz* on television was their inspiration. They created the scarecrow."

"Amazing," said Gerhart Malz.

"An adversary worthy of you, Mr. Malz," said Jupe.

"What?" said Malz.

"You never knew that Mrs. Chumley wasn't happy with a student's copy of the Vermeer," said Jupe. "You never knew that she wanted to own the real thing."

Malz looked at the painting over the mantel.

"It was part of her bargain with the Burroughs couple," said Jupe. "She would keep quiet and they would take the paintings—all but the Vermeer. She wanted the Vermeer."

"Good heavens!" Malz went to the fireplace and looked closely at the picture. "Well, I'll be!" he exclaimed. "It *is* the one from the museum. I should have spotted it right away. But what happened to the copy?"

"It was burned," said Jupe. "I found a few bits of canvas in the fireplace. I have them in a paper sack in the kitchen. The painting you see is the one that was taken from the museum today. How strange that you didn't miss it when you identified the other pictures at the harbor tonight."

"I—I was upset," said Malz.

"No, you weren't," said Jupe. "Actually, you did spot the picture here earlier this evening. You couldn't fail to spot it. That unfaded strip of wallpaper around the frame is a dead giveaway. That's what tipped me off to Mrs. Chumley's involvement in the robbery. It showed that a smaller painting was now hanging on the wall and protecting less of the wallpaper from fading. I knew the original Vermeer was smaller than the student copy. So I deduced Mrs. Chumley now had the painting from the museum—which she could only have gotten by being in league with the Burroughs couple.

"You had to have seen the picture was smaller, Mr. Malz. You had to have known it came from the museum. Yet you said nothing."

"I was too disturbed by the robbery to notice anything!" said Gerhart Malz.

"On the contrary," replied Jupiter. "You were amazingly calm after the theft. People who have been bound and gagged and locked in closets aren't usually so calm. So I started to wonder about you—and the painting."

"I—I was upset," said Malz again.

"After Mrs. Chumley fled, I examined her

picture closely. The paint on the canvas is still a bit tacky. It hasn't dried to the hardness that old paintings have.

"Mrs. Chumley didn't notice. She probably never handled the picture herself. And Burroughs and his wife were too busy to notice.

"Mrs. Chumley risked everything she had for the original Vermeer. Perhaps she was tired of living in someone else's house and looking after someone else's family. She wanted something really first-rate for herself. What she got was a forgery!

"And since *she* got a forgery, Mr. Malz, isn't it reasonable to suppose that many of the pictures stolen today are forgeries—excellent copies done by a man who can imitate the style of any painter?"

Jupe caught his breath and went on.

"You were going on vacation on Friday. I think you were going to take the genuine masterpieces with you and leave forgeries in their places. After today's theft, you wanted to keep things calm. You didn't dare draw attention to Mrs. Chumley's smaller painting. Someone might notice it was a fake instead of the original.

"When the other paintings were retrieved from the Burroughs couple, you didn't dare report the Vermeer missing. You'd have started a hunt for it that would have ended here in Mrs. Chumley's room. You knew you could slip the original Vermeer back into the museum. With luck, no one would be the wiser. No one would have any reason to suspect the authenticity of it or the other pictures.

"But you haven't had luck. Now the pictures will all be examined by experts. You'll be exposed. Where are the original paintings from the Mosby collection? In the apartment you keep in Santa Monica?"

Chief Reynolds went to the picture hanging over the mantel. He touched it, looked at his fingers, then turned to Malz. "We'll get a search warrant," he said.

Malz glared at Jupe. "You rotten kid," he said.

Jupe ignored him. "It's ironic," he said. "Burroughs and his wife went to endless trouble to commit their crime. And what they got was a beautiful collection of fakes. But how could they have known that a master forger had been there ahead of them?"

23

Mr. Hitchcock Reads the File

"It is reassuring when justice triumphs," said Alfred Hitchcock.

The famous motion picture director sat in his office with a file that Bob had given him open on his desk. He nodded approvingly at The Three Investigators. "You are to be congratulated," he said. "Not everyone would have suspected that two sets of criminals were working on the same crime at the same time. Of course the methods differed greatly. However magnificent the tunnel to the Mosby house was, it must have been clumsy compared to the work Gerhart Malz did on the imitation masterpieces."

"It was difficult to tell the originals from his copies," said Bob. "Now I understand why museums insist that students make copies that are a different size than the original!"

"Quite so," said Mr. Hitchcock. "Well, I am

delighted to have the opportunity to read the file on the case of the sinister scarecrow. I'm not at all surprised that The Three Investigators were involved in the doings at the Mosby Museum. Indeed, I would have been astonished if there had been a crime of such magnitude so near Rocky Beach and you had not been there."

Bob smiled. "Chief Reynolds says we have a talent for trouble."

"A doubtful asset," said Mr. Hitchcock, "but without it, life might be quite dull!"

Mr. Hitchcock closed the file and handed it back to Bob. "I shall be happy to introduce this new adventure for you," he said, "but there are a few questions I should like to ask. For example, how did Burroughs and his wife succeed in persuading an English lord to give them such a glowing reference?"

"Burroughs' real name is not Burroughs at all," said Jupiter. "It is Smith."

"Oh, no!" said Mr. Hitchcock.

"Yes. Robert Smith. His wife is Evelyn Smith, who was born Evelyn Baldridge. The couple have had many aliases. They are thieves with long records and international reputations.

"They were on a flight from England with a couple named Burroughs who truly were houseman and cook to Lord Armiston. The real Mr. and Mrs. Burroughs were planning to retire to Florida. They changed planes in New York. Mr. and Mrs. Smith decided that Lord Armiston might give them an excellent reference if they ever needed employment in a large household. They made a note of the name and went on to Los Angeles.

"Perhaps they had already started to lay plans to rob the Mosby Museum. Certainly they didn't waste much time. They were at the employment agency in Beverly Hills within a week of that airplane flight from England. The police have checked the records at the agency and learned that the couple who presented themselves as Mr. and Mrs. Burroughs refused several jobs that paid more than the one in the Radford house."

"But they could have waited months for an opening at the Radford place," said Mr. Hitchcock. "Perhaps there wouldn't have been an opening for years!"

"They could have gone to any of several homes in the Los Angeles area," said Jupe. "Burroughs—or rather Smith—had a list of dozens of places where there were jewels or works of art worth stealing."

Mr. Hitchcock sighed. "Foolish of him to keep such a list, but we are all capable of folly. And he was already taking a chance. Lord Armiston might hear from the real Burroughs and wonder about the inquiry from the employment agency."

"That did happen," said Jupiter. "Lord Armiston contacted the agency the day before the theft. The agency called Mrs. Chumley and warned her that her houseman and cook might be impostors. She said she didn't care—that she hadn't had such good help in years!"

"Unfortunate woman," said Mr. Hitchcock. "They had her completely in their power."

"She brought it on herself by pretending to be a cripple," said Jupiter. "But you can't help feeling sorry for her. She was picked up by the police in Santa Barbara. She had run out of gas there and was trying to pawn a ring to pay for more. She had left the house with absolutely no identification, and the pawnbroker became suspicious and called the authorities."

"What will happen to her?" said Mr. Hitchcock.

"I don't think she'll go to prison," said Jupe. "Her age is in her favor, and she has no previous record. Letitia Radford is paying for a lawyer for her. Letitia may be arbitrary and temperamental, but she's not a vengeful person."

"I should say not," said Mr. Hitchcock. "Under the circumstances, she is being quite merciful."

"Her encounter with the scarecrow seems to have changed her," said Jupe. "She has announced that she is not going back to Europe. She is going to stay in Chaparral Canyon and hire her own servants and really be the head of the house. She is even talking of doing volunteer work at the medical center at U.C.L.A."

"In short, she's growing up," said Mr. Hitchcock.

"One thing hasn't changed," said Pete. "She still jumps and screams if she sees a bee. I bet she'll never get used to bugs!"

"Speaking of which, what about Charles Wooley?" asked the director.

"He's still there, working on the hillside with his ants," Jupe reported. "And Ben Agnier is the pool man again."

"Very good," said Mr. Hitchcock. "It sounds like a satisfactory ending to an interesting case— interesting and unusual."

"You said it," Pete declared. "I can't ever remember tangling with a scarecrow before, and I hope we never do it again!"

"I wasn't referring to the scarecrow," said Mr. Hitchcock. "I was referring to the fact that you lads have seldom had so many suspects—and never have so many of them turned out to be guilty!"

ALFRED HITCHCOCK
and The Three Investigators Series